Sin City Kilts

SOUL OF IRON

JANUARY BAIN

Soul of Iron
ISBN # 978-1-80250-536-8
©Copyright January Bain 2023
Cover Art by Kelly Martin ©Copyright May 2023
Interior text design by Claire Siemaszkiewicz
Totally Bound Publishing

This is a work of fiction. All characters, places and events are from the author's imagination and should not be confused with fact. Any resemblance to persons, living or dead, events or places is purely coincidental.

All rights reserved. No part of this publication may be reproduced in any material form, whether by printing, photocopying, scanning or otherwise without the written permission of the publisher, Totally Bound Publishing.

Applications should be addressed in the first instance, in writing, to Totally Bound Publishing. Unauthorised or restricted acts in relation to this publication may result in civil proceedings and/or criminal prosecution.

The author and illustrator have asserted their respective rights under the Copyright Designs and Patents Acts 1988 (as amended) to be identified as the author of this book and illustrator of the artwork.

Published in 2023 by Totally Bound Publishing, United Kingdom.

No part of this book may be reproduced, scanned, or distributed in any printed or electronic form without permission. Please do not participate in or encourage piracy of copyrighted materials in violation of the authors' rights. Purchase only authorised copies.

Totally Bound Publishing is an imprint of Totally Entwined Group Limited.

If you purchased this book without a cover you should be aware that this book is stolen property. It was reported as "unsold and destroyed" to the publisher and neither the author nor the publisher has received any payment for this "stripped book".

Totally Bound Publishing books by January Bain

Brass Ring Sorority

Winning Casey

Chasing Lacey

Romancing Rebecca

TETRAD Group

Racing Peril

Racing the Tide

Racing the Whirlwind

Manitoba Tea & Tarot Mysteries

Magic, Mayhem & Murder

Movies, Moonlight & Magic

Moonshine, Magic & Murder

Sin City Wolf

Howl

Hunt

Honor

Hellfire

Sin City Kilts

Heart of Stone

Soul of Iron

Collections

A Little Bit Cupid: Lovestruck

SOUL OF IRON

Dedication

Thank you, dear reader, for choosing my story in this busy world. I appreciate it more than you can know.

A special thanks to my esteemed publishers, Claire and Rebecca, for their awesome support and standing behind this series that I am so excited to share with all of you.

To Rebecca, my brilliant editor and a woman I am honored to call friend—as always, bless your heart for making my stories shine.

Many thanks to all the staff and writers at Totally Bound Publishing.

To my very own White Knight, Don. How can a simple thank-you ever be enough? It's an honor to be with you. All my love, always.

Chapter One

What is the most cunning of all animals? That which man is yet to see ~ Indian proverb

Calan

The night wind lashed the casement windows of Castle Creigbourne, driving rain against the tower's glass. The din woke me from a battle I was winning, striking down the enemy with my mighty claymore that I'd named Slayer. *They don't accuse me of having an iron soul for nothing. I never give up, and danger's my life's blood, even in my dreams.*

Stretching, then grimacing as the numerous cuts and bruises from my recent cage fight made themselves known, I checked the time. Five a.m. *Early enough to avoid company.* I treasured time alone, a rare commodity in the Creig clan.

My bleary vision was made worse by a pounding headache curtesy of a night spent in our local pub celebrating the Burryman and my earlier knockout victory of a worthy opponent. I rubbed my eyes, blinked and spied my cell phone lying by the bed, reminding me of the encrypted email I'd gotten last night.

Right. Today my attendance was requested at virtual council. More like demanded, but also to be expected as my clan's enforcer and one of a select team of experts that composed the Worldwide Security for Lycans or WSL. The position was made for me…when I didn't have a damn hangover. Well, a good run across the moors would clear my head of the remaining cobwebs.

With no thought to dress, I strode naked from the room and took the stairs leading to the outdoors two at a time, exiting from the back of the keep. The scent of heather and moss stirred my senses as the rain ceased and a rainbow appeared over a rise in the land. I transformed to my other nature, entering through the glimmering doorway in the dimension next door, then exiting the portal as wolf. That split-second moment in time when my energy shifted, then reformed, exposing my wild nature, never got old.

On my massive paws, I loped across the wet green fields of Eilean maddah-allaidh or Wolf Island, eager to patrol our vast holdings and check for any interloper or breach of security. No one who knew of our piece of off-the-beaten-path real estate took the chance of riling one of us, the Highland Heathen Clan born of Wulvers and Vikings and ancient warriors, but I still kept a sharp lookout for the unexpected.

Someone finding our shores and causing havoc could not, and would not, be tolerated. The freedom of our heritage needed to continue, and I would protect my clan and our secrets to my dying breath. It explained why I'd chosen to live my life on my own, not willing to allow another to suffer if it was cut short.

Not that I intended that to happen, but in this world, shit happened.

I was halfway across the island when my nose picked up a scent. I skirted the area, recognizing the perfume of a woman best left to her own devices. Last thing I needed was giving Sherry, a cousin with whom I'd shared a mutual love of fine whiskey in the pub last night, any hope of us spending time together, old friend or not.

The longer route took me past Wulver Cave, and I slipped inside to quench my thirst. I had a secure location that no one, not even my clan, was aware of in the Highlands. I keep it fully stocked and ready in case of a need to evacuate my entire family at a moment's notice. Thankfully to date, there had been no need for its use.

At the edge of the underground freshwater lake, a feature of Wulver Cave, I peered around, making sure I was alone and not about to be ambushed by one of my brothers or cousins. It would be just like them to sneak up on me and try to pin me down. *As if.* It would just lead to a fight, then a standoff, something my headache could do without, though the fresh air was helping it fade.

I bent to lap the water with my tongue, then stilled as a vision appeared on its mirrorlike surface. *Danger.* An unknown wolf. Strange stripes marred its back. I swung my massive head around but there was no presence behind me or anywhere in the cave. *It was a warning then.* But where was this wolf? This interloper? Lachlan was the one of us blessed with second sight. This was normally his domain, being first born. Why was I being shown the image? Perhaps being enforcer, it was sent to me to aid in protecting my clan?

Grateful for the advance warning but growling with deadly intent over there being a threat somewhere that needed answering, I left the cave. I needed to speak with my brothers, warn them.

In the shadow of Castle Creigbourne, I shifted back to human and strode inside, prepared to shower and dress before tracking down Lachlan and Logan, and ten minutes later I entered the huge kitchen, spotting my quarry breaking their fast.

"Morning," Lachlan said, the intensity of his glance his normal modus operandum.

Logan was too busy stuffing his face to bother looking my way. The baby of our family, he was all about fulfilling his own physical needs first. *Spoiled doesn't cover it.* I might have been left to my own devices the most, being the middle child, but I was glad of it. I had a duty and commitment to my clan that few, if any, could match. My brother was studying film for heaven's sake, hardly the kind of pursuit our ancestors would have agreed with.

"Out patrolling again?" Lachlan asked.

Logan shook his head. "You know you don't have to do that, right? Waste of time in my opinion. No one in their right mind would attack us here."

"And what if they're not in their right mind?" I answered. "You just going to pretend psychopaths and usurpers don't exist?"

"Better than thinking something's hiding behind every rock, bro."

"You got something to say, spit it out, Logan."

"I think you've said enough, Logan," Lachlan, the clan's alpha admonished him. "What's up, Calan? You seem even more paranoid than usual. Something going on?"

I sat down across the expansive table from the pair and dove into the pancakes, sausages and eggs, a morning favorite. "Yeah, something's going on all right," I said after swallowing a bite of the food I'd piled my plate with.

"Something do with that lass I saw you drinking with last night?" Logan asked, slipping in a zinger from another angle. Incorrigible summed him up. I pitied the female that tried to straighten him out. Or maybe I pitied him more, for what female would put up with him? I did envy Lachlan and his female Esme. A perfect pairing and one that would keep them happy and blessed for their whole lives.

"I love them and leave them, bro. No other way for it," I answered.

"Me too. I just prefer to acknowledge that one might be my Forever Mate," Logan said. "Maybe I'll get lucky like Lachlan."

"Not bloody likely. No she-wolf would put up with the likes of you. She'd need a lobotomy first," I said, enjoying the instant look of anger that replaced Logan's customary smugness.

"Better than needing a heart or soul, Iron Man." Logan pretended my hit hadn't landed.

Or maybe it didn't—he was so full of it. Well, confidence cannot be underrated, though true bravery in battle was of far more vital importance than interactions with the opposite sex, in my opinion.

My Iron Man tag, which our clan tied to the warrior god, Lugh, of Celtic fame, beat Logan's Aengus, male god of love and youth, all to hell. Though on second thoughts, as someone had to continue our bloodlines, it had best be someone not heading into danger at every opportunity. An image of my best friend Galen rose, reminding me of the downside of being an enforcer and making my heart squeeze for the devastating loss to his family.

"Let's finish up. We've got that council meeting in five minutes." Lachlan glanced at the clock.

His words woke me from thoughts I would prefer to avoid and normally managed to keep squashed down flat in the back of my mind.

We got up and made our way to the library where all virtual meetings took place, in front of the big screen. Lachlan fired up the equipment and locked onto the weblink.

"Good tidings from the Highland Heathen Clan to the Houses of Luceres, Anche and Ribelle," Lachlan said as the three alphas came on stream.

Polite interactions out of the way, Cristaldo, of the House of Luceres, the most powerful and rich family of werewolves in America, spoke first, as was his right.

"There's been a disturbing incident in the desert just outside Vegas. Someone got sloppy and was caught on video shifting of all things! I don't have to tell any of you of what vital importance this is to security. In the interests of all Lycans, we need to squash this video. Now. We've never been exposed like this before. No one knows how we really shift, only gathering their intel from books and movies. This shift was the real deal."

My heartrate jacked up. This was bad news. I wanted to throttle the culprit. "Any leads on who made the recording?" I jumped in. *So, the vision in the cave holds merit.*

"A person with the online tag of Miracle. Don't even know if they're male or female. So far, the video's only been posted on the dark web. But this needs addressing now."

"I'm leaving now," I said. "Expect me ASAP."

No one disagreed with me, of course. This was my express domain.

"I'll have someone meet you when you arrive, Calan," Cristaldo said.

"Have the other members of WSL been alerted?" I asked. If not, I'd call them in as needed.

"No, we called you first."

After the meeting concluded and the video feed had been turned off, Lachlan turned to me, suspicion clear in his green eyes. "You knew something of this?"

"I was going to tell you I saw something in Wulver Cave before His Highness interrupted." I jerked my head in the screen's direction. "A strange wolf with unusual stripping on its back." I shrugged. "That was it, nothing else."

"I know you can be trusted to get to the bottom of it, Calan. Go with my blessing."

"Mine too, bro," Logan said. And for once he did look sincere. Well, when push came to shove, we did stick together.

No one had better badmouth one of our clan, if they knew what was good for them.

Chapter Two

Mira

After throwing the fresh meat into the fenced compound, I plunked the bucket down on the cement. Though my job as the newest hire as a zoologist at Vegas Zoo called for more administration duties than feeding ones, I liked to get out and stay in touch with the animals at least once a week To see if their habitat needed improving the old-fashioned way by observing them.

It was important to stay in touch with all aspects of running a zoo, not just fund raising, budgeting and public relations. My cell phone rang as the big cats began to prowl across the ground, headed for the chunks of food I'd tossed. They looked magnificent in the dying light, all sinew and tawny fur, casting long shadows. Animals I understood and respected, their nature controlled by instinct. No crime in that. *But people – don't even get me started.*

I didn't recognize the number when I tugged my phone out of my shorts and hoped it wasn't another one of *those* calls, demanding repayment of my brother Evan's drug debts. I didn't have any more spare cash this month than last. And no way to contact him since he'd done a vanishing act a month ago, just like our father did before he was born.

My mother, who'd died last year and Deadbeat, the name I'd given to the guy I unfortunately shared DNA with, hadn't even bothered to make it legal. I missed my mom terribly, but it was my brother I worried about, angry as I was at him for drop-kicking me under the bus…notwithstanding his note to say he would be back when the heat died down.

Funny, but drug dealers, much like loan sharks and other nefarious characters, don't take no for an answer. The thought of more taint being added to our family name made me even more determined to make a name for myself. The dream of being listed in the hallowed halls of scientific discovery loomed large in my mind, pulled a little closer due to recent developments. *No, make those incredible recent developments.*

"Hello?" I said into my cell.

"Good day. I'm calling from Stone, MacDonald and McGuire on behalf of Mr. George MacDonald. With whom am I speaking, please?" a woman chirped,

"What's this in regards to?" I asked, suspicion of what they were after or wanted from me making the hair on the back of my neck rise.

"If you are indeed Miracle Camile Tala, as our records indicate, we will need to set up an appointment for you to come in to speak with Mr. MacDonald as soon as possible. When would be convenient for you?"

I sighed. "It's Mira and I have a job. I can't just drop everything without knowing what it's about. Could you at least put George MacDonald on the phone?"

The lions were gorging themselves not twenty feet away from me, with the occasional keen stare in my direction as if sizing up my potential as food. I wouldn't turn my back on them or anyone else, for that matter. *A gal's got to watch her own back in this day and age.*

"He's busy at the moment, but I can have him call you?"

Figures. Too important to make his own calls. "What kind of business is Georgie in?"

Her tone turned to ice. "We are a respectable law firm right here in Vegas."

Might as well get this over with. "Fine. I have plans for tonight, but I can swing by in half an hour if that works for you. Text me the address."

Ending the call, I caught a slight movement out of the corner of my eye at the perimeter of the fence line. I squinted. It was difficult to see in the twilight, but it looked like a huge wolf with darker stripes on his back and haunches. The look of the feral creature slinking so near me chilled my bones and I gave a shiver. Was it the same wolf? Had it tracked me down after my recording it two nights ago in the desert?

The memory seized hold of my brain, making it race with the impact of such a find. Was my secret passion for cryptozoology about to be fulfilled with the discovery of a species of wolf thought to be extinct, the long-lamented Tasmanian wolf not sighted since 1933?

Had it become a true cryptid? The amazing, mind-blowing transformation I had bore witness to, when after a burst of intense light like a portal or rent in the atmosphere, a large, darker complexioned man had appeared in the wolf's place. The creature had definitely undergone a metamorphosis right in front of my unbelieving eyes, all recorded on my iPhone.

Prove this definitively, capture more footage and make a record of essential facts, and my name would be made in the best circles, stamping out my shady background in one fell swoop. Hell, maybe I'd even pick up some cash prizes that would help with Evan's debt.

* * * *

Forty-five minutes later and running late after leaving detailed reports on the animals under my care for the morning crew, I was striding into Georgie's impressive law offices.

"I'm Mira Tala here to see George MacDonald."

The administrative assistant, Judy Murray, as the sign perched on the reception desk read, gave me a professional smile that did not reach her coolly assessing gray eyes. I was glad that I had taken the time for a quick shower and put on street clothes instead of my usual shorts and T-shirt. A simple dress and pumps suited this rarefied atmosphere.

"Yes, we talked on the phone. If you would have a seat, please, I will let Mr. MacDonald know."

Instead of sitting, I walked over to the bank of windows that faced the street. The late-day traffic was heavy, cars and trucks whizzing by. Why was everyone always in such a hurry? *Rushing from traffic light to traffic light like they fancy themselves NASCAR drivers.* Someday, when my life was sorted and my name made, I wanted to find time to smell the roses. *But not for a long, long time.*

I wasn't like my few friends who had left the rat race behind for marriage and family. More like out to pasture, with their constant harping on what they'd left behind, on the rare nights we'd managed to get together this past year. Like Holly and her constant complaining about not even having time to shower let alone write a single word for the Great American novel she was always going to pen now that she was home to do so, having left a lucrative position in the publishing industry to raise a brood.

No, marriage and responsibility existed in a distant land and one I was not visiting anytime soon. No man could possibly be worth giving up my dreams for. I agreed with my best friend Amy, who was also out to make a name for herself, sharing that she had no plans for romance, marriage or kids in the near future.

"Mr. MacDonald will see you now," Judy said, interrupting my thoughts.

I ventured down the hallway to the open door she'd pointed out and knocked on the doorframe to alert the lawyer to my presence. The middle-aged man with the silver-fox coiffured hair glanced up and, catching sight of me, frowned.

"Come in."

I took immediate offense that I was a problem he would prefer not to be dealing with. Someday people treating me like this would be a thing of the past. And what did this man have on me that warranted him looking pissed at seeing me, anyway? I could only imagine it had something to do with my family. Though how anyone of them could afford a lawyer of this caliber remained to be seen. It would take a few years before my salary increased to the point I could even pay off all my school loans.

He stayed seated at his meant-to-be-intimidating desk and cleared his throat as I stood in front of him.

"What's this about?" I lead with, tapping one leather-soled shoe on the hardwood floor, which made a satisfying and annoying sound. If I'd had a ballpoint pen, I'd be clicking it to make my point.

"You have proof with you of who you are?" he asked, his dark eyes beady behind his glasses.

"I do," I said.

"Would I be able to have a look at it?"

Unable to come up with an excuse, I sighed and pulled out my driver's license and held it out to him to inspect, not letting go of it.

"Thank you," he said and flicked open a file. "You are the daughter of LeeAnn Tala and Michael Caruso?"

I nodded. "What's this about?"

"I've got the last will and testament of Michael George Caruso here."

Has Deadbeat died? A sudden flush of emotion surprised me and not in a good way.

"My apologies on the passing of your father." He glanced at me, a trace of sympathy visible in his expression. "Would you care to sit down?"

I sat primly on one of the three office chairs perched in front of his desk. Had Deadbeat left me something? Or Evan? Any extra cash would be welcomed to apply to his growing debt. The vig or interest on loan debts was far steeper than going to a bank, I had discovered to my dismay. Going to a loan shark would be my last resort if Evan didn't come back to town soon.

"To my daughter, Miracle, I leave all my worldly possessions."

George held out a key with a bedraggled tag attached, pinched between his thumb and forefinger.

"This unlocks a security facility at the address written on it."

"Did my father pay you to take care of this for him?" I asked, taking the rusty key. There was no mention of Evan because Deadbeat had fled before he was born. But if anything of value was set aside in storage, we'd divide it equally. Though that was a longer shot than winning the lottery. "Because I don't have any money at the moment and arrangements would have to be made."

"That was taken care of long ago, back when this law firm first began, when my father started it as a sole proprietor and would do most anything to obtain clients. You don't owe us anything."

So, that had caused the lawyer's haughty attitude toward this current duty. But I was relieved I owed them nothing and it did explain why Deadbeat could afford the cost. A struggling law firm was a cheaper bet than the prominent business it had risen to since. I imagined the security facility I held the key to in my sweaty hand was filled with junk, stuff that I would just have to throw out to avoid paying any more fees to the facility. Probably another bill awaited there for past rent due. Or maybe it had already been cleaned out and someone else's stuff was housed there now? None of the scenarios promised anything more than extra grief on my part.

"Okay, then." I whirled around to exit stage right, clutching the key so tightly in my fist it burned my palm. The sooner I got out of here, the quicker I could get to my dinner. I'd missed lunch, but taking care of animals always took first priority.

"Ah, I wish you good luck," George said.

I barely heard him on my way out of the door. *Don't worry, I make my own damn luck, Georgie.*

In front of the law offices, I threw the key in the recycling trash bin near the door. There. I hurried to my old beater, my heels clicking on the cement. Sitting inside the too-hot vehicle, I dithered for a moment. What if the storage facility actually contained something useful? Maybe a diary that explained something of why Deadbeat had abandoned us. *Shit.* I should at least check it out.

I hurried from the car and back to the recycling bin and dug the damn key out of the garbage. A part of me was dead certain I would be sorry for doing this. That I was making a huge mistake.

Chapter Three

Calan

I sat in front of the imposing desk, facing Cristaldo. In person the shifter was even more imposing, leadership riding easy on his Armani-clad shoulders.

"*Let your plans be dark and impenetrable as night, and when you move, fall like a thunderbolt.*" I quoted Sun Tzu, from *The Art of War*, to make my point. A good quote saved words.

"Good. Then we're in agreement." Cristaldo nodded, his perfectly coiffured hair barely moving. "You'll squash this episode and report your findings to the Tribunal."

"No need to call in the entire team at this point. I'll do the recon, then assess what's needed," I said with a shrug. "This whole thing should be history in no time."

"A history I want eliminated from the books. Humans are untrustworthy, so there's no telling what direction things would take if we're proven without a shadow of doubt to exist. You're authorized to do whatever is deemed necessary to eliminate this threat."

I nodded. "I understand. I'll be in touch."

We shook hands and I took my leave. *Time to go to work.* Ignoring the looks of patrons and staff alike, I strode through the casino, intent on making quick work of things. *Track down this Miracle Tala and, if they won't see reason, take care of them.* It was the old way of things and necessary for this situation, but not something I would find any enjoyment in.

I'd gotten the perp's real name through my contacts. The WSL had a well-paid group of individuals hand-picked for their special skill sets. *Tech super abilities can never be underrated.*

In the parking lot, I spied my ride. A black Mercedes SUV I had requested specifically not to draw attention. I had also chosen to dress down in a white linen shirt and black dress pants leaving my usual kilt and accessories at home. Slipping in behind the wheel, I brought up the address for Mira Tala on the GPS. From what little I had gleaned about the person, they normally kept a low profile. Why they had to chosen this time to go almost public with a damning video was anyone's guess. That had to be stopped before things progressed any further.

Not wanting to confront the person just yet or alert them to my presence until I had a better idea who I was dealing with, I parked a mile away from the rural property that the suspect had rented a few months back, and exited the vehicle. I would shift and reconnoiter the area. If they weren't home, I'd break in and discover all I could. *Nothing like a good background check to assist in getting to know the enemy.*

Shedding my clothes and shifting to wolf under the newly risen Vegas moon, I headed for the fence line, my night vision enhanced by my animal nature. The scent of a strange wolf lingered in the air and on the urine splashed on desert fauna, firing the hackles on the back of my neck. What was this? Who was the interloper? Nose to the ground, I followed the vile odor all around the edges of the property. The wolf had been tracking the human inside. What did it mean? Was this the wolf exposed on video? Were they as upset as other Lycans? Hmm, maybe they intended to take care of the problem themselves.

A slight twinge of sympathy for the doomed human panged, but I quickly pushed it aside. This was no time for emotion. What was at stake was too important.

The farmhouse appeared deserted, with only the porch light left on. It was easy enough to shift and head inside. In human form once more, I discovered an unlocked window, shook my head at the resident's incompetence and made my way inside. The place was spartanly furnished, just an odd mix of cheap furniture. I made note of that. The person might be able to be bought off if nothing else. Money to remain quiet could be a powerful deterrent, but it would depend on what the motive was for wanting to expose our species.

I shrugged in disgust. *Money and fame.* People were far too predictable. Not that there weren't good humans. More often than not in my opinion. *Just why use us to make your way in the world?*

I rifled through the mail left on the kitchen counter. Bills. Lots of bills. This Mira person was in debt. An answering machine attached to the landline phone drew my attention, and I replayed the messages.

"You know who this is and you know what you need to do. You have twelve hours. We clear?"

I growled at the tone of the caller. A loan shark or drug dealer seemed the probable speaker of such words. What kind of person got themselves into such deep trouble?

Picking up a photo from the coffee table, I viewed the image of a beautiful young woman with amazing red-gold hair smiling for the camera, her arm around a younger male teenager of the same coloring. *Brother and sister?* My vision kept returning to the pleasing smile of the female, so alluring and free of guile. Could this possibly be the Miracle I was searching for? She didn't fit the profile that had been growing in my mind since I'd been on the case. I needed to check this out. I wished I had my iPhone to snap a photo of the arresting image but, being naked, that was out of the question. I picked up a pink sweater on the sofa and held it to my nose. *Hmm, a very pleasing scent as well.*

The sounds of a vehicle coming down the lane alerted me to company. *Time to get a move on.* I climbed back out of the window and shifted to wolf, then loped across the backyard to the fence. I jumped the fence, moved into a better position for observing and settled down on the ground to wait for the person or persons arriving.

The compact red Smart Car pulled to an abrupt stop in front of the house. A small human female jumped out, her bright blonde hair that was neither red or gold but a lovely shade in between pulled back from her pretty face, shining under the moonlight. Miracle Tala? She unlocked the door and hurried inside. Her scent came on the scant breeze and I breathed it in. That same pleasing scent that was on the article of clothing. If this was Miracle she was certainly not what I was expecting.

Time to do a little more investigating. Check in with our contact here in Vegas and have them look up her driver's license. See if the photos match.

I raced through the desert to my parked car, redressed and got busy on the onboard computer, sending off my encrypted request. Within minutes, I had my answer. Yes, Miracle Tala was indeed the pretty female. A zoologist of all things. The file of known facts on the young woman aged twenty-five was short. I had insisted on knowing things as soon as possible after all, but a longer file would soon follow.

Just as I was admiring her graduation photo from a local university, the red car from the farmhouse earlier began barreling toward me. I ducked down out of sight just as she flew by the spot where I was parked on the side of the road. Where was she headed in such a rush? Maybe the dire message on the machine had something to do with it? I certainly couldn't let her go meet with *that* person without some backup.

I kept the Smart Car in my sights, tailing her through the twisted backstreets of Vegas. She pulled up in front of an industrial-looking complex. The overhead sign indicated it was a storage compound, open all night. Parked on the front street, I watched her head into the office. In a few minutes she was back out and marching down the sidewalk toward a vast row of units, each fitted with a garage-type door.

Time to go find out what she's up to. I strode into the office, watching the security guard's eyes widen at the sight of a huge man dressed in black pants and white shirt darken his doorway.

"Evening, sir," I said, smiling to lessen the middle-aged man's anxiety. For some reason I had that effect on other males. They either wanted to be my friend or fight me. Well, a few had run away as well.

"Hello," he said, returning my smile. Business came first then. Good, I could work with that. And the fact that he was not the owner, judging by the faded uniform. This guy could use some extra cash, working nights in a storage facility.

"I'm wanting to rent your units."

"Units? You want more than one?" The man's dark eyebrows raised toward his graying hairline.

"Yes, and maybe I could have them situated close to that young lady you just spoke to?" I pulled out a thick bundle of folded hundred-dollar bills and set them down on the counter. "I can make it well worth your while. I just wanted to meet the young lady—nothing nefarious in my intentions, I promise you. You can watch everything on CCTV, right? Prove my intentions are honorable?"

The man's eyebrows vanished under his hairline at the sight of so many greenbacks. He cleared his throat and nodded. "Just so happens there are a number of units quite near that location...in fact, only ones that are left empty at the moment. How many do you want?"

"All of them, and, if you can dispense with the paperwork, and just give me a key to one that's nearest hers, I'll be out of your way. Oh, and an empty box would be most helpful."

"Done." The man pocketed the cash, grabbed a key and handed it to me along with a large cardboard container. "Here you go. Nice doing business with you."

I exited the office with the box and drove to the back of the compound. The one thing that perturbed me about the recent transaction was what if I were the bad guy and that guard just handed over a way to nab an innocent victim? Of course, he would be watching, no doubt of that. The compound was well covered by cameras.

I parked my car near the series of newly rented units, wanting to meet the intriguing Mira Tala, needing her to see reason, if nothing else than to save her own hide.

Chapter Four

Mira

The key slipped in easily enough, then, when I twisted it to open the lock, it kept sticking. Frustrated, I pushed at a strand of hair that had slipped from my ponytail. I had changed back into shorts and a white T-shirt to make my self-imposed task easier. I didn't want to head back to the office, defeated, so I put my back into it, pushing hard, praying I didn't break the damn key off in the lock.

"Can I help you, lass?"

The nice rumbly voice with the wonderful cadence of a Scotsman came from my right, and I whirled around. No one had been there only seconds ago, but now a very large man stood directly in my path. A good-looking man also—some might even say extraordinarily handsome—with his long light brown hair pulled back in a tie at his neck. He even smelled good.

Surreal didn't cover it. Was I hallucinating, maybe? Gone back in time like that heroine from those *Outlander* stories? *Do hallucinations include all the senses?* I could see him, hear him, smell him. I reached out and touched his arm, just to make sure. Yup, he was as firm and as hot as he looked. Well, that just left one sense. Taste. I licked my lips.

His eyes widened, his gaze dropping to linger on my mouth. "What seems to be the trouble, lass?" He repeated his question.

"The key won't turn in the lock," I said, finally finding my voice.

"Here, let me try." He dropped the cardboard box he was carrying on the ground and came closer, touching my shoulder with his arm. His closeness sent a shiver racing through me and I stepped back.

"I hope there wasn't anything breakable in there?"

"What?" he asked, distracted by working to turn the annoying key.

"You know, in the box you just dropped."

"Nothing breakable. Ah, there we go. You're in, lass."

He gave me a big satisfied grin and my breath stalled for a full second. *The guy should be in the movies, he'd have women's hearts aflutter in no time. Men's too, probably.* I hoped he wasn't gay though that wasn't the vibe I was getting.

"Thank you, Mr…?" I nudged.

"Calan Creig at your service, lass."

"Mira Tala," I said and stuck out my hand. "You've been a lifesaver, Mr. Creig."

"Calan, please." His hand swallowed mine and the jolt of electricity between us sparked. His eyes widened.

We held on a bit longer than normal before letting our hands drop awkwardly to our sides.

"Can I help you move or carry something?" he asked.

"I don't want to hold you up." *Yes, I do.* "You've helped already and you must have stuff to do."

"I always have time for such a charming lovely lass," he said, his white teeth flashing in his tan face.

"Well, thanks, but I'm just going to take a look around. I recently found out about this place, having been left a key in a will."

"You inherited it?" he asked, his gaze penetrating.

Thoughts of my mom and Deadbeat filled my head. "Yeah." I shrugged. "No biggie."

"Well, I'm sorry for your loss," he said.

"Thanks. Maybe I'll see you around. You know, when you come to visit your stuff?"

"I'd be happy to hang around. Maybe we could grab a coffee or something?" he asked. "I'm right next door." He held up his key with the number attached. It indeed was for the next unit. *Could it really be this easy? Meeting a real hunk at a storage facility?*

"Well, maybe?" I said, not wanting to seem too eager. Fate was never this kind. Something must be off in the universe tonight. Maybe the full moon held some magic for Mira Tala for once? *Yeah, right.*

Calan opened the door for me. "After you, Mira."

And a real gentleman. Maybe this was to make up for the horrid month I had been having keeping the bad guys at bay? Well, if it was, I'd take it. Something about Calan said he was trustworthy. Maybe too good-looking for his own good, but someone I could count on. It was a lot to take in about a stranger on first meeting and it made my head reel.

The air inside the unit smelled musty and stale, overheated from the Vegas relentless sunshine. How long since anyone had been in here? I sneezed three times in quick succession. Even walking stirred up the dust.

"Bless you, Mira."

"Thanks. You should go—it's so dusty and dirty in here."

"It washes off. So, what are you looking for?"

"I don't know really. It belonged to Deadbeat."

"Who's Deadbeat?"

I flushed. "The man whose DNA I unfortunately carry. I even had to pay out of pocket to come in here to find all this junk." I shook my head, my eyes still bleary from sneezing. Soon as Mr. McHottie found out about my situation, he'd go running into the woods. Who could blame him? My situation was complicated, as they say.

"Well, maybe there's something here of value?" His tone was as skeptical as my thoughts. He began opening boxes, surprising me. His mere presence took up a lot of space in the fifteen-by-ten room. "You might find some old antique or painting worth something. According to the internet, that happens more than you think."

"Yeah, right. My family's never had anything worth any value in its entire history." Now why was I spilling my guts to a complete stranger? Was it just because he was the hottest guy I'd ever met? A woman in her right mind wouldn't let an unknown acquaintance go through her things. *Guess that only proves I'm not in my right mind.* Truthfully, it may have been sometime since I had been. With Evan on the lam, and the over-the-top experience of finding a possible cryptid, I was in an unusual place for certain. One thing though, if Calan could put up with me now, he was a keeper. *What!* Why was I thinking such crazy thoughts?

Embarrassed, I moved in deeper, batting at cobwebs to keep them off me.

"Say, this is interesting." Calan held up a tightly wrapped, transparent package of something that looked like small cloudy crystals.

"What's that?" Intrigued, I held out my hand to inspect the item.

"Oh Lord, it's a box of crystal meth. Drugs." He didn't hand it over but threw it back in the box, his face contorted by dismay.

Shocked, I looked down into the box. It held six of the eight-by-twelve by three-inch packages. "Oh my God, that's a *lot* of drugs."

"Keep your voice down," he warned, his eyes flashing a brilliant green, riveting me, and we locked glances.

Horrified, I closed the lid of the box. "So, this is what they want," I said, not thinking.

"Who wants?"

I rubbed my aching forehead. How had I gone from the frying pan into the fire so quickly? Hold on, maybe this could work out? If I traded the drugs for the debt owed, I could get my brother off the hook. He could come home. I needed him—even with his addiction, we had good times together. And he was my only family. The problem was, I couldn't stand the idea of putting drugs back on the street. That was just wrong. Damn it, I was no closer to fixing things than before. Actually, things seemed to have gotten worse. Other than meeting Calan.

"I guess I have to get rid of it," I said, as tempted as I was to trade it for Evan. Family was family and I loved my brother dearly, all his faults aside. But enough to compromise my ethics and deal in drugs that could harm so many other people?

"You're not certain?" Calan looked at me sideways.

"It's complicated, but yeah, I'm certain. It's the right thing to do." Even if it would mean freedom for Evan.

"What are you not telling me? Is someone trying to pressure you?" He looked outraged now, like he wanted to go out and be my protector by throttling somebody. *Strange.*

"You should go. This is my problem." I stood back and gave him a serious look of intent. "I don't want you having any trouble over this. If this gets out, well, let's just say its not going to be pretty."

He frowned. "I can't leave you like this. You got too much on your plate as it is."

"How would you know anything about me? I'm fine. I can take care of things myself. I aways have. Please, just go." I didn't need the distraction of Mr. McHottie while I figured out what to do. Mainly, how to dispose of the drugs without getting caught.

Calan looked reluctant, then reached in his pocket and handed me a gold embossed business card. "If you need anything, please call. This is my personal cell number. You can reach me anytime."

"Thanks." I took it and shoved it in my shorts without looking at it.

"Okay, then. Nice meeting you, Mira. Maybe we can get together for a drink soon?"

"Yeah, maybe. After I take care of some things."

Chapter Five

Calan

I had intended the interview to go vastly different than it had. But before I cautioned her about spreading any more information about her find, I needed to dig up what was going on with her. Inheriting a stash of drugs was insane. And why the strange attraction between us? I had been bowled over when we shook hands, a fire racing through my veins in a most unexpected manner. *What was that about?*

If anyone needed watching over, it was Mira Tala. She was in deep trouble right up to her eyebrows. I couldn't let this go. I had to help her. *Tonight.* Time was of the essence in this situation.

I paused outside the storage space I had rented and fiddled with my phone, waiting for her to come out of her unit. I considered a few ideas, preparing for however this would go, even if I just ended up bundling her into the SUV and hauling her ass—fine as it was, and I had taken a necessary moment to notice—away.

Five minutes later she emerged, dragging the box filled with the drugs with her.

"Let me help you with that," I said, stepping up.

She looked up at me with surprise, her face pink from exertion. "I thought you'd gone."

"No, just answering some work emails." I easily picked up the container. "Where do you want this?"

"In the back, please, if you can get it in."

Her expression most likely mirrored mine. I shook my head. "I don't see this fitting."

I tried, but it was a few inches too big for the space. "I'll drive it wherever you want it to go," I said, knowing how insane that sounded. But if I could pull this off, it was the perfect bribery item to secure her cooperation.

"I can't let you do that…you know…with what's inside," she stage-whispered, her expression wide-eyed and concerned. *For me.*

Another vehicle began making its way toward us. I made an instant decision and hit the key fob to open the boot of the Mercedes, securing it. "There. Now, where do you live?" I asked, like I didn't already know.

The sedan passed us by, turning at the end of the row and vanishing from view.

Mira looked nervous, like she expected the police to show up at any moment. Thank goodness I had come along in the nick of time.

"I live over on Brentwood Road, on the outskirts of the city. Just follow me." She didn't look happy about it, but she had no choice. Alone with her, back at her house, I would have more ease to deal with this situation.

Slipping in behind the wheel, I watched her get into her insanely tiny car and start it up. I shook my head. No way would my six-four self fit inside. All us Creigs are extra-large, something that commanded respect even before we demonstrated our innate ability to lead or assist others.

With the drugs in the back, I drove the Mercedes at the correct speed, making sure to avoid committing any traffic infractions. Not that I was that concerned. I would try cash first, then call our contact at police headquarters if that failed. But I preferred to avoid the aggravation. I was on a short timeline—I needed this situation fixed yesterday.

Twenty minutes later and we turned into her driveway. I parked near her vehicle, scanning the area. *No sight of any interlopers.* I opened the trunk and hauled out the box of drugs.

"Thanks for doing this."

"Where do you want them?" I said, striding up to her front door.

She unlocked the door and gestured inside. "On the kitchen table for now."

"You'll need to find a better hiding place than that," I remarked as I headed inside. I caught another whiff of her tantalizing fragrance. What was it? *Light floral like violets with an undercurrent of sweet musk that is all female.* "Does this place have a cellar?"

"It does. But it's so dark down there I don't tend to go there much."

"Get a torch and lead the way," I instructed. "Best to hide this right now until you can dispose of it. It's a ticking bomb if anyone discovers you have it."

"Right…a torch is a flashlight."

I watched her pull a silver torch from one of the kitchen drawers and switch it on, checking if it worked.

A new plan came to me. "Soon as its dark, I'll dig a hole and bury it."

She chewed at her bottom lip. "That makes sense. But I can't ask you to do that. You're dressed way too nice and you've been such a big help already. I'll dig it myself."

"Mira, I'm twice as big as you and many times as strong. I can dig a hole much quicker and the sooner it's done the better." I had the upper hand in the situation just by spouting common sense.

She frowned. "I can pay you for your time."

"A drink and some dinner would be more than enough payment," I said, adding a charming smile. What was I doing? Now I was trying to charm the lass who needed a good stern warning more than anything? Bribery or blackmail were the next options on my list to secure her silence.

Her expression cleared. "Sure, I have the ingredients for pasta and a salad. Even some garlic toast. Do you like Italian food?"

"I love all food."

She smiled and the sun came out. "So, the way to your heart *is* through your stomach," she teased, one hand on a curvy hip. She was one of those women who didn't seem to realize how beautiful they are. Little makeup, hair in a ponytail, shorts and a T-shirt, she took my breath away. Now, if I could just talk my way into her bed instead of having to protect her by sleeping in my car, the night would end perfectly.

She led the way toward the back of the house and opened a door in the hallway. "It's down here."

I followed her down the steep steps, her flashlight unnecessary with my keen eyesight. I laid the box on a table, noting a shovel and rake leaning up against the cement wall. "Good, there are tools for later. I hope you have lots of hot water?"

"Why?" she asked, her pretty blue eyes widening.

"I'll need a shower after digging in the dirt and sand."

"Oh, of course."

I watched her swallow, her expression riveting. Her scent became stronger, overpowering the slight mustiness of the cellar air.

Damn, but the woman was as attracted to me as I was to her.

Chapter Six

Mira

I scooted out of the basement ahead of Calan. Bringing a complete stranger into my life was not me, but there was no way to fix this now. I could at least feed the man for taking the time to help me. Maybe fate had seen fit to send me a guardian angel man? *Yeah, right!* Though I was more than due for some good twist of fate, considering the stress of this past month.

Checking out the time on the clock over the stove, I made a quick decision, thankful I had shopped this week and had made a week's worth of meals the day before. I even had a container of my grandmother's favorite pasta sauce all prepared. "I'll start supper now. Would you like a beer or anything? I might have some wine."

"A beer is fine."

I pulled two beers from the fridge and handed one to Calan, who made himself at home at my small wooden table. I had to smile to myself as I watched him take a drink from the long-necked bottle while I set a large pot of water on the stove to boil. If I thought he appeared surreal showing up at the security site, he was twice that now sitting in my tiny kitchen. I reheated the homemade Italian sauce, threw the fixings together for a salad and popped the garlic bread into tinfoil and into the preheated oven.

In less than twenty minutes, I had everything on the table. *Not bad, Mira Tala,* I complimented myself. I knew my female ancestors would be proud.

"This looks wonderful," Calan said, looking impressed. "You always eat this well?"

I shrugged, a bit embarrassed by the intensity of his stare. My, but he had incredible emerald-green eyes. A gal could fall right into those dreamy depths if she wasn't careful. I looked away, busying myself with laying my white linen napkin on my lap. We might not have had much growing up, but mom had insisted on doing things nicely with stuff like proper cloth napkins at mealtimes.

"Most nights. I mean, you have to eat, right, so why not enjoy it? Please, dig in. No formality around here." I cooked for Evan up until the time he'd pulled the vanishing act, at least on the nights he was trying to be normal. The thought brought a lump to my throat, and I covered it by filling my own plate.

We ate in companionable silence, surprising me. When he was done, two extra helpings later, he patted his stomach and leaned back, granting me full view of his appreciation.

"So, Miss Mira Tala, what else do you excel at?"

Heat rose in my face. "Thanks, but it wasn't that much, just pasta."

"Please, tell me a bit about yourself." He checked the clock. "We still have time before dark. Might as well spend it getting to know each other…no harm in that, right?"

"Well…" I began to peel the paper label off my beer as I tried to collect my thoughts. Being so near Mr. McHottie, now that a fundamental requirement from the bottom of Maslow's hierarchy of human needs had been taken care, another was rearing its head. I pressed my thighs together to supress it. "I was born right here in Vegas though we were moved around a lot. Well, me and my brother Evan. Sometimes my mom had us leave in the middle of the night to avoid the rent collector."

"And Deadbeat, this man who left you the drugs is your father?"

Though I agreed with the look of disgust on Calan's face, I pressed my lips together to avoid expressing my displeasure at him, or anyone else for that matter, pointing it out. After all, Calan was doing me a solid. And did have the facts correct.

"Yeah. I think the anger that my brother holds for his father and his upbringing is why he's so messed up, why he got into drugs in the first place. He wants to make something of himself, but he feels he didn't get any of the breaks to do so."

"And yet you did, right? You made something of yourself. You are an amazing chef, that I can attest to. Now, I'm back to my original question. What else do you do well, Mira?"

"I work as a zoologist at Vegas Zoo. And I have a special passion on the side. One that may bring me money and fame." The excitement of what I had just discovered brimmed over, making me forget myself for a moment. "I'll make our family look good to the world yet, if it's the last thing I do!"

"That's important to you? Making your name in zoology?"

"No, it's more than that. I recently sighted what the world thinks is an extinct species, belonging to the thylacines or more commonly the Tasmanian wolf, not seen since 1933. Not only that, but here's the most interesting part—it seems to have evolved in a way that is beyond amazing. I videoed it and it shows a wolf, then a flash of intense light with the portal or entrance to another world visible, then a man appearing in that exact same spot a split-second later."

I jumped up and grabbed my cell phone, holding it out to show him the short video. "I know it's dark, but still, it looks real, right?" I hung over Calan's shoulder, his incredible scent filling my lungs with the scent of clean manliness plus a hint of musk that could drive a woman crazy, or to drink. "Want another beer?" I asked, moving away from him to open the refrigerator door.

"Sure." He smiled in agreement, then returned his focus to the screen. "Have you shared this with anyone else?"

I shrugged and hauled out two bottles of beer, handing one to Calan. "Just on my small private account on the dark web with other fans of cryptid sightings. Under an avatar. No one knows its me or would connect me to it. But I needed to share with someone that would understand my reluctance to go public without more proof. We do that all the time in our community. Keeps us all safe. Oh, and I did share with my best friend, Amy Stratton, but she'd never share it."

"So, you haven't posed this on regular social media at all?"

I frowned, confused. "No, why? I want to keep the find quiet until I have more proof. Bit early to make this public. That could be weeks or even months away. In the world of cryptozoology, it's best to make an exact science of it and have a proper report prepared from field records with no room for error or doubt first. Otherwise, you might be thought a crackpot."

"Hmm."

My guest appeared lost in thought for a moment. Suspicion reared its ugly head. Something was up and I needed to know what it was. "What's all this about? Why are you asking about a video being leaked?"

Calan stilled and my heart dropped. For a second, he looked about to say something, thought better of it, and just shook his head. "Nothing, just asking. Never met a woman interested in cryptozoology before."

"Why are you here in Vegas, Calan?"

"I'm here to help my aunt and uncle move. Plus, take in a few tourist attractions."

"Ah, that's why you were at the storage place," I said, things clicking into place. "What do you do back home? It's Scotland, right?" *Famous for kilts.* I could only imagine Calan in one, bare-chested, an ancient warrior strutting across the green. I licked my lips at the arresting image.

"Security. A group of like-minded guys that provide protection to those that need it."

"Like celebrities or important people?"

"Right. And what do you like to do for fun, Mira?" He leaned in closer over the table and my vision wandered to his lips. They looked so inviting, well formed and plump.

I shrugged, taking a sip of my beer before answering. "Not much time for that. I'm pretty busy between working at the zoo and working nights on my thesis. Plus trying to look out for my brother, Evan."

"No boyfriend?"

"No. I got way too much to do to give up the time necessary to make one man happy." Then I realized how that sounded, and backpedaled a bit, making a small joke. "Not that there's anything wrong with that. But I've watched some of my friends fall for a guy, get married, have kids, then bemoan the fact that they don't have the time to follow their own passions."

"So, you don't think a woman can have it all? A husband, children and a fulfilling career?"

He seemed very interested, so I continued to make my case. "None of the women I know seems to have managed it. Maybe if they had a nanny, or more help from their husbands, but the load still seems to fall on the female."

"In your opinion."

"More than just opinion. The facts speak for themselves. I don't put words in my friends' mouths."

"I think one can have it all if they are willing to compromise, schedule and plan. Mates should share the load, make sure the other's needs are being met. The Creig is a fine example. I think she'd like you, having so much compassion for a family member. She pretends to be so hard, but when it comes down to it, she's got a huge heart. She's had an incredible life. Fought for us as matriarch and head of our clan, raised three beautiful children, two boys and a girl, and followed her passion for painting landscapes. Made a good name for herself in art circles. And she's also a patron of the arts and heads many charities. She's of the mind that it's a matter of deciding on a course and going about it one day at a time, without losing sight of the big picture."

"She sounds like one in a million. I'd love to meet her. But no way could I live up to that. I'd say she must have loads of money, right? Hired help to make her day easier. I did notice you drive a Mercedes." I tilted my head to encompass the yard outside. "And your clothes are expensive, that's obvious."

"I like nice things and I've earned them by working day and night in business. But yes, the Creigs are not hard up for money. Old money."

I peeled off more of the label on my bottle before my hand was suddenly captured in his. I swallowed and looked into his piercing green eyes, my mouth going dry though I had consumed two beers, my limit. His touch made the world drop away and I waited for what was next, my breathing hitched.

His next words disappointed me. "I'll see to burying that package now."

Chapter Seven

Calan

Why had I not used that opening to warn Mira of the consequences of exposing Lycans, now or in the future? I had the perfect bribery item, the drugs. But another part of me didn't want this to end on such a quick, sour note. Mira intrigued me, so vital and full of life, and yet so cautious to take any chances. She'd been hurt a lot—that was obvious, something I wanted to spare her now.

Plus, I had a bigger problem at the moment. Maybe I should be grateful she'd alerted me to it. The Tasmanian. There was a reason they were extinct. The Wildmen had become so inbred that the last of them had turned insane. *Only out for themselves. The human equivalent of a sociopath in the werewolf world.* They'd had to be stamped out by civilized weres. And if a new one had somehow escaped notice until now, he or she had to be dealt with. The threat level with a Tasmanian on the lose was considered extreme.

Question was, how or why had it come to the USA from Tasmania, an island south of Australia, their last known beachhead? And what did they expect to gain?

I carted the box of drugs and digging tools to the farthest corner of the property, far from peering eyes. As I dug, I mulled over how best to approach the situation. Anything I said now made me look bad. Like I was only here to take care of business, when in reality, it had become more than that. Far more than that.

My attraction to the alluring female in trouble up to her eyebrows was something I had never experienced before. *Give me a band of brothers to lead anytime.* This, however, was brand-new territory. A minefield. My attraction to Mira was extreme, and that could only mean one thing—something else was going on.

A streak of anger shot through me, making the dirt fly as I applied my shovel to the hard packed earth in pissed-off frustration. *It couldn't have been just a sweet meet-cute-and-we're-at-it kind of fun. No, it had to be this insane minefield of extending circumstances that could blow up in my face at any moment.* Well, nothing for it but to make her feel such passion for me that when and if everything was revealed, she'd not give me a ton of grief.

If only she was a she-wolf, it would be so much easier. She'd have been schooled in how an alpha male and a female partnering worked. She'd have understood the extreme lust that was difficult to near impossible to hold at bay, under certain circumstances. Not that rape was ever involved, but a mutual attraction led to the kind of depth of romantic entanglement that humans could not imagine having.

If I'm really smart, I'll run for the hills right now. But I can't do that. My need to protect a vulnerable female precluded all common sense.

There. The hole was deep enough. I shoved the box into the space and began piling soil on top of it. After packing the earth down hard again, I dragged a tumbleweed over it to disguise the disturbance of soil. I marked the spot with my mind, knowing that at some point, this would have to be dealt with further. Picking up the shovel again, I stalked back toward the house in the distance. *Time for a shower.* A scent drifting in on the scant breeze stopped me dead in my tracks about fifty yards from the residence.

Damn it, the Tasmanian. Loaded for trouble, judging by the foul odor the loathsome creature emitted with every slimy step. Was this fortuitous or a disaster in the making? I needed to make sure to lead him well away from view before attacking. Otherwise, exposure was a possibility, with Mira looking for any opportunity to record more about the extinct species. The last thing I needed was to be videoed transforming to wolf. I'd never live it down.

I crept through the underbush of sage and cacti, making sure to avoid twigs that could snap and alert the demon to my presence. Back at the edge of the property, I circled around, headed in the right direction judging by the direct assault to my olfactory senses. When was the last time this foul creature had a bath?

The full moon emerged from behind the clouds, exposing even more of the landscape. Yes. There was the culprit, slinking through the fence, headed my way. The hackles bristled along my neck and back. The bastard was a menace, coming near Mira like this.

This ends now.

I threw off my clothes and charged directly at the offender, shifting to wolf through the multiverse in a split-second while running full bore. Knocking into him head-first, my snapping jaws just missed his throat by scant millimeters. I twisted mid-air, coming right back at him, charging his flank, looking to gain a grip on his rough, disgusting hide.

The slash of long claws, the sounds of a death battle, stirred the desert air, sending all other creatures diving for cover. We circled each other, searching for a weakness. The Tasmanian's eyes shone red—devil red. He had the desperate, desolate look of a loner, a Nomad without a pack. Dust rose into the air as our huge paws gained purchase and disturbed the sandy soil, like bulls in the death rings of Spain.

The interloper kept his belly close to the ground, afraid to expose his vulnerable underside. I leapt onto his back, digging my claws into his shoulder, his cries of pain echoing in the darkness. He twisted his head and nipped at my foreleg, holding on like a dog with a bone.

I used my extra weight and size to jerk him sideways, causing us to cartwheel in the dirt, bodies locked in deadly combat. He shook me off, and I took a slash to my leg. Watching for any opportunity, I leapt for his jugular at first chance. But he tore away, blood dripping from the wound and darkening the ground. He was weakening from blood loss—I read the fatigue and shakiness in his stance. He needed to get away and lick his wounds. But I wasn't having that. I wanted to end this here and now. *Protect the woman. End the threat.*

An owl hooted in the distance, a harbinger of death and change, just before the sounds of an approaching siren rent the air. The Tasmanian took the opportunity to turn tail and run. Reluctant as I was to leave unfinished business, I had to let him go. Something else was afoot that required my immediate attention. If that police car was turning into Mira's driveway, that meant the man at the security facility couldn't be trusted. No—the siren faded away as the police car continued on its journey. *Thank God.*

I took a quick look around for my discarded clothes and re-dressed in short order. Ignoring my bleeding wounds that I hoped wouldn't be too apparent, I limped hurriedly to the house, realizing the coward had bitten into my Achilles tendon and it would need time to heal.

Nearing the residence, I heard Mira call out my name. Seeing her framed by the shimmer of the overhead yard light, her beautiful hair glowing, her expression concerned, made my worries about her personal safety only deepen. A gorgeous female living alone in the desert was a ticking bomb, especially with her baggage.

"You're hurt!" she said, rushing to my side.

"It's nothing." I shrugged. "Just slipped up with the shovel. You can quit worrying—it's well hidden where no one will find it." *Except me.*

"Thank you. This whole thing…you've been such help. Come, I need to look at those wounds." She tugged my arm over her head, drawing me in nice and close. I should get hurt more often, if this was the result.

I breathed in her delectable essence, her scent flooding and overcoming my common sense as I allowed her to help me inside. Why not, it was the most enjoyable action I'd encountered so far on this trip.

"Sit," she directed, pointing at a chair. She bustled about, opening a cupboard next to the refrigerator and hauling out a first aid kit.

"Yes, ma'am."

"Don't *ma'am* me. I'm far too young."

"And far too pretty," I said, giving her a wink that I wished would make her panties drop straight to the floor. Hurt or not, I was a man of action, and nothing took the mind away from the odd twinge or two of pain like making love with a ravishingly beautiful woman.

Then I remembered something that made me hesitate. To be one hundred percent certain a mate was the only one for a wolf, especially a Wulver, they needed to join bodies, as proof lay in the extreme nature of the pairing. The impulse to rush her and take her to my bed fired my imagination, and it was all I could do not to act on it. *Not my best idea.* I didn't need or want a Forever Mate, much as I desired to bed Mira right now. A smart wolf would walk away. Now. But I needed to guard her, see this to a conclusion, so I had to stay, like it or not. And I liked it too much for comfort.

"I'll bet you say that to every girl you fancy," she said, pulling up a chair close to mine.

"You think I fancy you?" I teased, allowing her to remove my shirt to check for wounds. "A female who cooks like an expert chef, is kind enough to bandage me up and looks like an angel?"

I enjoyed watching the pink rise in her cheeks as her lips quirked upward. "These look more like claw marks that a falling out with a shovel head." She inspected the shoulder wound, frowning. Then those devasting blue, blue eyes met mine and my heart skipped a beat. Yup, apparently it happens to alphas too. Another check mark on the score card for her being someone I should not be tangling with.

"I scratched myself on a bramble."

"Rather deep for that. And you were limping. Did you sprain your ankle as well?" she asked in an accusing tone.

"Slightly." She didn't need to see my leg. What if the bite was obvious?

"I need a shower before it's wrapped," I said, diverting her attention away from her possible discovery of my being chomped at by a wild animal. The very wild animal she was seeking. The one that I was now certain was stalking Mira. How was I going to alert her to the danger in a way that left me in the clear? Or maybe I was overthinking this? Just say I was bitten by a wolf stalking her property. But then what? How would she take that? I didn't know her well enough to predict her actions. She might be the kind to want to rush out and film him, putting herself in danger. Or report it to some agency. The last thing I needed was more exposure.

"Fine. I'll apply ointment and bandages after you wash up. No point before then."

I stood up and offered my hand, pulling Mira to her feet, stilling myself for the rush of lust bound to follow. I could never sully her with the residue of the damn Tasmanian DNA that lingered on my skin. "Lead the way."

She pulled a pair of large bath towels from the linen closet in the short hallway and handed it to me. "In there." She pointed at a closed door.

"Thank you. Be back soon, gorgeous. Don't start without me."

"Start what?" she asked, her eyes darkening, pretending innocence at the attraction that scorched the very air around us and was impossible to miss, for human or wolf. A sense of time coming to a complete standstill, the outcome important, added a level of intensity that made my body vibrate with want and need to seal the deal. No way was I going to start this, but my mouth had other ideas, the words spilling out before I could hold them back.

"You know." I strode into the bathroom and left the door open as invitation. Yeah, common sense had left the station. Good thing I had the strength and determination of ten men, honed via long experience as enforcer of my clan and elite member of the WSL.

I showered quickly, wincing as the driving water hit my open wounds, flushing the blood down the drain. Turning the water setting to ice cold, I stood under its punishing effect's in efforts to shrink my overwhelming desire to bed Mira. It helped for a bit, making me shiver as I dried myself.

The wound on the back of my ankle did indeed look like an animal had taken a chomp out of my flesh. I opened the medicine cabinet and found a small packet of band aids, perfect for camouflaging the area. I also applied them to my chest where the devil's claws had sliced the skin. *Best I fix up myself, then stand guard during the night, leaving Mira to toss and turn in her bed alone.* That was the smart thing to do. The right thing to do, and the most difficult.

I exited the bathroom with a towel tied tightly around my waist, needing to get a fresh set of clothes. Padding down the hallway and into the kitchen, I kept a sharp eye out for my lovely hostess.

Opening the boot of the Mercedes, I pulled out a second set of clothes encased in plastic, then re-dressed quickly. It would be far easier to avoid temptation in a suit of amor, but Armani would have to do. I slipped back inside the house and there she was, looking at me with surprise.

"I thought I was going to tend your wounds *before* you got dressed," Mira said, her voice accusing me of not sticking to the plan.

I shrugged it off. "All taken care of." Werewolf wounds heal so easily and quickly, it would be difficult to explain if she were to see them just a few hours later.

"Would you like a nightcap?" she asked. The way she said it suggested I would be leaving soon.

Her cell rang, interrupting the moment. Maybe I needed to pretend to get drunk, spend the night on her couch? Because no way would I be leaving the fair Mira alone. Not with gangsters pushing her for money, drugs hidden on her property and an insane psycho Tasmanian on her trail. It was obvious she was the innocent victim in all this and had no idea how much trouble she was in.

Chapter Eight

Mira

When I checked the number on my phone, I winced and hoped Calan didn't see my unease. He'd already done more than enough for me tonight, but talk about poor timing. Here was a gorgeous male specimen, the like I had never met before, standing in my kitchen, looking like he just might be interested in me, and now the bad guys had to butt their heads in again. Against my better judgment, I declined the call and smiled brightly at Calan.

"About that drink, what's your pleasure?" *I know mine is to jump your bones, sooner rather than later. I mean, how often does such a prime specimen enter my sphere? Like never.*

He pursed his lips, like he had questions, then seemed to think better of it. "Whatever you're having is fine. Say, I got a bottle or two of Scotland's finest in my trunk. Would you care for some fine Highland whiskey?"

"That sounds grand."

I watched Calan leave via the back door, once more mesmerized by the incredible way the man moved, with such amazing animal grace, like he could stalk prey and conquer any situation. I'd never met a man built like that. I shivered, imagining him turning all that power my way. He'd been teasing me earlier…did he mean it? Did he really want us to jump into bed?

I'd had little experience with the opposite sex, having spent most of my life studying animals. But really, were we that much different? I snorted. Not much, we were just a bit more intelligent about hiding our wants, that was all. And I knew what I wanted, though I would be voted least likely to have a one-night stand by those that knew me well.

The man of the hour was back in a flash, a golden bottle of what looked like top shelf liquor held in one of his fine hands. I blushed, wondering if the rest of him was as well formed.

I pulled two tall crystal glasses from the cupboard and set them down on the counter, then watched Calan expertly open the whiskey. I didn't recognize the brand, single malt whiskey, Macallan Lalique, whose fine fragrance permeated the air. Of course, his own scent was far more alluring. I stepped back a bit to allow him the space to pour. When he handed one to me, our eyes met and the moment electrified me beyond the pale. Yup, I was sunk if this continued. Trouble was, I wanted to be sunk, to forget the events of the day more than anything. Had fate set this man in my path?

"What shall we toast?" he asked, handing me a glass.

"To meeting a new friend," I said. "You've been so kind to a complete stranger. I can't thank you enough."

Something passed through his eyes. *Regret?* Uncertain, I took a swallow of the liquor and enjoyed its heat, its mellow flavor tantalizing my tastebuds and warming my belly.

"Say, this is a fine drink," I said to cover up the awkwardness.

"To friendship," he said at last, before drinking from his glass.

"Come. No need to stand. I do have a rather comfortable sofa in the living room."

"Lead the way."

Calan's presence in my house seemed to be looming even larger, if that were possible. He gave off such an alpha vibe, as if the world were his and he strode the planet with impunity. This awesome, unbelievable and strangest night of my life had made me far more aware of what my life was missing. Someone to spend the celebrational times along with the grittier times with. I mean, the guy had stepped up, helped me in the most amazing way and all it had cost me was a meal that I didn't have to eat alone. And now he'd just introduced me to the finest whiskey I could imagine drinking. Too bad this couldn't go anywhere. He was here on vacation while I had a ton of work to do.

"We need music," I said as Calan settled his magnificent self on my sofa. I was being more spontaneous that I had been in a month of Sundays. I turned on my iPod in its speaker box, setting the play of songs to random. Sometimes its fun to see what fate choses.

When the sexy, throaty voice of Diana Krall hit the air, my stomach took a tumble.

"Great voice." Calan set his whiskey down on the coffee table. "Let's dance, gorgeous."

This time my stomach took a joy ride. I swallowed nervously. "Sure, why not." *Well duh, because my body and his will be pressed close together to some sultry music meant to send two people spinning off between the sheets.*

He held out his hand, a magnetic look in those stunning green eyes that was impossible to turn away from. Then he slowly reeled me in with the come-hither crook of his forefinger, suggesting a landing place on his broad chest. In mere seconds, I was snuggled against that warmth, listening to a strongly beating heart. His scent was even more captivating up close and enveloped me with a cloud of tantalizing pheromones that seemed to know exactly what they were doing—reeling me in one full breath at a time.

We danced pressed tight together for a few minutes. The long, lingering song need never end, in my opinion. The words of love lost and a yearning for its return spoke to me on the most elemental of levels. To all lovers that never stood a chance or a prayer. I understood their pain.

I knew it the moment before it happened. As the song drifted toward its close, Calan was going to kiss me. I'd bet everything I had on it. It was my last rational thought before his head bent toward mine, and I pulled back from his chest just enough to allow him access. Then the rest of the world vanished as he tightened his hold on me and pressed those inviting lips to mine. When his tongue slipped along the crease, awakening every nerve ending, I softened, allowing him to explore my mouth. He took immediate advantage, thrusting inside to tangle his tongue with mine while I gave back every moan and nuance of arousal.

It was so damn good, beyond amazing, kissing the insanely attractive man in my living room. My entire body throbbed with need. Calan brought his hands up and pushed them into my hair, his fingers working to loosen my braid while he kissed my mouth, my cheeks, my eyelids with such passion that my heart fluttered. I didn't want him to stop, to have this incredible sensation ever end. It felt like a dream, an insane moment in the universe when two ready bodies demanded more, so much more…

"Where's your bed?" he asked, his voice rough now, demanding.

He bore me up in his arms in one swift maneuver that left me reeling. I rested, light as a feather against his solid frame. Never had I felt so feminine, so *necessary* as I did at that moment. He was my warrior, the man from legend that had stepped out of a storybook to invade my life. I wanted him, more than I wanted anything ever before.

I opened my mouth to speak when a series of loud poundings erupted on the back door, halting Calan in his tracks. More jarring noise came as the door was slammed into by something unseen, sounding like it broke right off its hinges, thudding to the floor. Then the noise of boots thundering in the hallway. I couldn't believe my ears. What the hell was going on?

Calan set me on my feet and pushed me behind him, confronting the pair of home invaders as they burst into the living room.

Through a haze of shock, I stared dimly at the villains that had invaded my personal space. Calan didn't look nearly as worried as I thought he should be when I recognized the two thugs. These were the men my brother owed money to.

The bigger of the two, the one I knew as Big Joe, took a fighter's stance, a gun suddenly appearing in his hands. The other, Scarface, had the prerequisite knife slash from his right eyebrow to his chin, scaring pretty much everyone he met. Frightened to my core for not only me but my guest, and angry at myself for bringing Calan into this terrible danger, I could only stare at the despicable gangsters.

Why had I not answered that call earlier tonight from them? It was my fault, just wanting a little time before having to deal with the real world, enjoying that little bit of fairy tale I had been given this night since my rescuer showed up. Now it had escalated and Calan was in mortal danger. That seemed even worse than my own dire predicament. The man was innocent of any wrongdoing, just helping me out of the goodness of his heart.

"Where's the money, sugar tits?" Scarface asked, his twisted countenance adding an edge to his demand. Big Joe held the gun on Calan, his expression suggesting he was begging him to just try something so he'd have an excuse to shoot him.

"I have a little saved. In my purse…in the bedroom. I'll get it," I said trying to pacify the pair.

"No need, Mira. They were just leaving," Calan said, mystifying everyone in the room. Then Big Joe burst into harsh laughter that held no mirth.

"Yeah, right. Not until we get what we came for, buster."

"Oh, you'll get what you came for and more," Calan said, his voice turning so deadly as he calmly promised repercussions that I could do nothing but stare at him.

The guy had it going on. Even the pair of punks that faced us looked a bit taken aback.

"Calan, I owe these men some money. I don't want you involved," I pleaded, staring down the black barrel of the gun still pointed at us and thinking of all the damage it could do to the beautiful flesh of the man at my side. He'd already been hurt once tonight on my behalf, burying the drugs.

"I'm not one to back down, Mira, but I think these *gentlemen* and I should take this outside," he said with a nod to the two gangsters. The way he said *gentlemen* left little doubt to what he wanted to call them.

"Not going to happen, asshole. We're taking what we came for. Either in funds or trade. Her choice."

I swallowed my fear and loathing. *Evan, what were you thinking, not paying these men?* It wouldn't do to rail at my brother—he was a victim of his upbringing and weaknesses. But I had eighty-one dollars plus change in my purse, not enough to make even a dent in the interest owed.

"I think you two had better be going now. But first, you owe Miss Tala an apology for breaking down her door. And payment to fix it."

The two thugs looked at Calan like he had grown two heads while I could only shake mine.

"So, what do you say? You going to cease and desist, or do I have to show you the door?" Calan asked. He spoke to me then, not looking away from the two invaders. "Be ready and run."

What was he going to do? He had no weapon on him. That I would known from our dance. Was he some kind of martial arts guru? *But nothing trumps a gun.*

Big Joe gestured with the black and silver pistol, his expression impatient and hate-filled. "Listen, fucker,

I'm the one holding the gun. What I say goes. Now, money or the woman? Your choice."

"I've already told you my choice to take this outside," Calan said with disdain.

Suddenly the gun went off with a blast, like Big Joe was sick of negotiations and wanted to prove the weapon was loaded. Instead of running away, I froze, shocked to my core again at the level of violence in my own home when just a few minutes before I was experiencing the kind of kiss that makes a woman's pussy sit up and take notice.

"Run!" Calan said, before rushing the man, knocking into him and driving him to the floor. The gun flew away, under the sofa where it lay hidden in the dark. I watched in horror as Scarface jumped on Calan from behind. This was so wrong, two against one! I looked around frantically and spied the baseball bat my brother had left standing in the corner of the room. He kept a weapon in every room, just in case. I grabbed it with determined fingers and turned back to the battle.

Calan was an amazing fighter, I spotted that right away as I hesitated, waiting for an opportunity. Both the gangsters were getting a sound thrashing. Sure, the furniture was being destroyed as the men knocked into my shabby-chic pieces, but my white knight was obviously winning the day.

When Scarface tried to crawl away with Calan hot on his tail, Big Joe took the opportunity to attack Calan from behind, coming at him with a leg broken off the end table. That was when I raised the bat and let him have it. A huge thud on the shoulders to stun him made the gangster drop onto his face and belly, the fight knocked out of him for the moment.

A whirl of movement, a blur that was almost impossible to see with the naked eye and suddenly both criminals were tied up together, back-to-back. *Impressive.*

Calan had hardly broken a sweat I noticed, as I gave him a shaky grin. I felt empowered by helping him take the bastards down. But then I thought of who I was dealing with and the hard realization that the boss would only send more minions to do his bidding took the shine out of the moment.

"I thought I told you to run," Calan said, a pointed arch to his fine eyebrows.

"I brought this on you. I couldn't not help." I set the baseball bat down. "I hate to say this, but I think this will only anger their boss. He'll send more."

"Damn right he will! He won't rest until—"

The rest of Scarface's speech was muffled by the sock Calan stuffed in his mouth. I let loose a shaky laugh, the adrenaline in my system spiking. For my efforts, Scarface gave me the evil eye and I hiccuped, realizing I had just made things worse for myself.

Calan's arms enclosed me, bringing security and warmth. "It's okay, lass. You're safe now. I'll never let them come near you again."

Scarface's murderous looks disagreed, but I tore myself away from staring at his ugly mug. It wasn't the scar that made it so unattractive, but his horrible attitude. I chose instead to believe there was still hope that all this would end. That was what standing there with Calan did for me. Gave me hope. Blessed hope.

"What are we going to do with them now?" I asked.

"Let me worry about that. I want you to pack your things. I'm taking you away from this situation right now—tonight. You'll stay with me until it's resolved."

I wanted to protest, to say I could handle it, but in truth, I did need his help. That was beyond obvious. If I stayed in this house, they would be gunning for me. By dawn more bad men would show up at my door, ready for revenge. Guys like that lived on their reputations and this incident screamed of intent to bring me to my knees. Make me pay for making them look bad, like the losers they were.

"Yes, thank you."

He gave me a final hug and a reassuring smile. "Go pack. I'll take care of these idiots."

I didn't bother to ask how. I just wanted them out of my house.

"Why are you being so nice to me?" I did end up asking. No man I had ever met would have done what Calan had done on my behalf this strange, bizarre night. One for the history books.

Calan just gave a self-depreciating shrug. "It's not in my DNA to allow a female to be accosted by criminals. No way could I see a woman like you in trouble without doing something to fix it." He gestured at the two men. "I'll make sure this never blows back on you. That I can promise."

Again, I didn't ask how, instead striding from the room to grab a bag.

Chapter Nine

Calan

While Mira left the room to pack, I grabbed hold of the pair of tethered idiots and hauled their sorry asses out through the back door. I marched them straight across the yard to the fence line, then pointed at the horizon. They didn't have a clue between them of how lucky they were that Mira was there to bear witness. Otherwise, they'd have met my wolf and likely not lived to tell the tale. "Vegas is that way. But if I were you, I'd head for parts unknown. Once your boss hears of your failure to follow orders, you may find yourselves in difficulties."

I pulled the socks from their mouths, taking some delight in knowing they would be trekking barefoot across the scabby landscape sure to prickle those tender tootsies.

"Aren't you going to untie us?" Scarface asked, his expression woebegone.

"No. You can darn well figure out that part. It's only a mile to the nearest gas station. I'm sure they'll sell you a knife or cutting tool there."

"You are going to be in a world of hurt when the boss hears of this," Big Joe said, his expression gnarly.

"You can tell him from me that if he dares show his face anywhere near Mira or her brother or sends anyone else after them, he can kiss everything he holds dear goodbye. And I don't make promises I can't keep. I belong to a small group of elite assassins, and they will come gunning for you. We clear?"

Of course, I didn't belong to a group that arranged murder for hire, but they didn't know that.

Both sets of eyes widened at my warning. Then the pair stumbled off into the darkness, grumbling and swearing at each other, presumably unhappy about their lot in life. Crab walking to the gas station was going to be a bitch. I made a one-eighty and headed back to the house. Mira was now my entire responsibility, and I was ready and prepared to protect her, with my life if need be.

"What did you do with those guys?" Mira asked as she handed me her travel bag. "I'm taking snacks for the road." She began to rummage through the cupboards.

"I let them hike home. They could use a cooling-off period."

"Surprised you didn't throw them in the trunk of your Mercedes and drive them even farther into the desert. I wouldn't blame you—they shot at you! Oh my God!"

She grabbed hold of the counter, her whole body trembling with emotion. I quickly set down the bag and hugged her from behind.

"I'm fine. We're both fine." I kissed the back of her bare neck. God, she felt and smelled like heaven on earth.

Her body softened. I wanted to take her to bed, right this moment, wrong as it would be considering the lies and mistruths that separated us. *But no time.* We needed to get out. *Now.* My biggest fear that loomed like an albatross around my neck was Mira finding out about my heritage before I could explain things. Though how I was going to manage that was anyone's guess. All I could do now was protect her, keep the innocent woman safe from the despicable men that walked this earth and wanted to do her harm.

A siren began screaming again in the distance…and getting louder and nearer.

"Damn! Now what?" I growled and grabbed Mira's arm. "Let's get out of here before something else happens."

I didn't need to ask her twice. We rushed outside and dove into the Mercedes. I threw her bag in the back seat and fired the motor. She was already seated next to me, her expression alert.

"Buckle up," I ordered and we made a screeching U-turn in the yard before tearing off down the driveway.

Sure enough, a Las Vegas Metropolitan Police Department black and white SUV was driving down Mira's lane, its strobe light flashing. And damn it, a police dog sat waiting impatiently in the back of the vehicle, meaning a drug search would soon be underway. Someone had called the cops on Mira. Who? Most likely culprit was that creep at the storage lockers. *Bribery only gets you so far these days.*

"Maybe we should stop?" Mira asked, her expression worried.

"Not a good plan. They could be fake cops. Hell, that's been happening more and more. Someone may have been alerted about the drugs and now wants to steal them. That box is worth a lot of money on the streets. Best we just keep going."

The driver of the police car had a determined look on his face. And damn it if he didn't play chicken with us. He turned the wheel of the vehicle and drove straight toward us.

"See, I was right. No real policeman would do that. Hang on!"

When he got closer, I jerked the wheel of the Mercedes and drove around the pair on two tires, making Mira and me list to the left, a fancy maneuver all my men in Worldwide Security for Lycans practiced.

We emerged behind the vehicle, and I set the Mercedes back down on four tires as smoothly as possible.

"Do you think they'll find the drugs?" Mira asked, chewing on a fingernail.

"Unlikely. And it's on the boundary between two properties, so that's in your favor." I didn't mention that I'd urinated on the spot to make certain that no dog would venture nearby. They'd give the drugs a wide berth. All dogs are terrified of our species, unless they'd been raised with us since they were pups.

I reached out and enfolded her soft hands in mine as they lay on her lap. "Don't worry so much. This will get straightened out, I promise."

"Who are you really, Calan? No normal man can drive like that." She shook her head in disbelief.

"Would you believe I once drove as a stunt driver for the movies?" I asked, wanting to lighten the moment. Her touch was electrifying my blood, making another part of my anatomy take too much interest in the outcome of this night. I adjusted my cock but stayed as hard as iron.

"How could they get here so fast?" she asked, abandoning questioning me, which gave me a bit of ease. Her amazing scent, heightened by her fear and arousal, drifted into my nose, reminding me of how precious she was becoming.

"The guy from earlier tonight had to have called it in. He must have access to cameras inside those storage lockers."

"That makes sense. And he didn't realize what was in that box until you opened it. Where are we going now?"

I eyed the road behind us in the rear-view mirror. So far it was clear that no one was following us. *Best not to take Mira to the Glitter Palace just yet.* I needed time alone with her, time to ease her into knowing the danger that exposing us created for her. "An out-of-the-way motel would fit the bill. Any suggestions? You know the area better than I do. Or we can look it up on the guidance system?"

"Turn right at the next intersection. I know just the place we can hole up for the night. The Bluebird Motel. It's out of town and a quiet location off the interstate. Not sure how they're surviving with so little traffic."

Though I could go hours yet without rest, or days, if need be, taking some time to figure a new plan was a good idea. And humans needed far more rest than werewolves. Part of Mira's paleness was due to exhaustion, no doubt. The thought of her tiredness made my cock soften a bit, at least enough to make it easier to think about other things.

We drove along the secondary asection of highway that Mira pointed out, the traffic light at the early hour, and I was relieved to see we weren't being followed. Just one night alone with her, and maybe after she'd rested and I was even further into her good books, I could explain some of my mission. I disliked lying to the woman. She was far too special for that, even if it was for her own good.

"I can't believe you and I just met," Mira said with a sigh. "So bloody much has happened. I hope it's not going to scare you away? I could use a friend that jumps in when its necessary."

Her quiet tone made my heart squeeze. *Yup, lying sucks.* And being placed in the 'friend' category was not exactly what I had in mind.

"No, I'm not easily scared. Not raised that way."

"Your life is an unknown to me. Soon as I've had a few hours of shut-eye, we should talk more," she suggested, leaning back in her seat and yawning.

In short order, tiny little snores began to escape her sweet lips, making me smile and shake my head. It was a little too nice driving along in the dark with the headlamps spilling circles of bluish light on the roadway, cocooned in the Mercedes with Mira. I'd better keep my head on straight, if I knew what was good for me and for my clansmen.

I spotted the Bluebird Motel a few miles later and turned onto the access road. The typical off-interstate motel, painted a fresh shade of medium blue, featured a neon sign with a flashing bluebird, one second sitting, the next with its wings upraised as if ready to fly away. *Not my usual choice of home away from home.* I thought of all the upscale hotels I'd stayed in that catered to the customer's every whim, no matter how odd or weird.

Old money with more wealth added every year made such decisions a no-brainer. Maybe I could treat her to a lavish hotel stay soon complete with a day spa. Right now, I just wanted to get her inside and let her sleep in relative comfort.

I shut off the motor near the small building marked *Office* and slipped out of the Mercedes, intent on getting the best rooms available. Mira barely stirred as I relocked the doors with the key fob to make certain she remained safe.

The office was empty when I ventured inside, the bell ringing over the doorway obviously set to alert the night worker. A young boy with excited hair filled with some grooming product suddenly poked his head around the doorway and spotted me standing there. He came fully into the room, his sleepy look suggesting he'd not expected company. Or maybe it was a family-owned enterprise, and he hung around in the back just in case of late-night business.

"I'd like to book all of your best rooms available," I said, pulling out my gold card.

His eyes widened at my request. "Sure, mister. We have lots of rooms left. Middle of the week is so quiet. How many do you want?"

"All of them," I reiterated without judgment. The boy had been woken from a nap.

The young man blushed, realizing what he'd asked. "We have five rooms open. They're kind of all the same, so I can't say one is better than the other. Will that do?"

I nodded. A *No Vacancy* sign would deter anyone else from stopping by. "Put them on this card."

His eyes opened farther at the kind of credit card I handed over. *Not a common one.*

"That will be one hundred and eight dollars a night, times five, so that will be five hundred and forty—"

"Make it a grand and throw in lots of ice, snacks and towels. Then I don't want to be disturbed until I report back in. Can you do that? Oh, and you never saw me. All right?"

"Sure, whatever you want, mister. Are you a spy or something?"

"No. But my lady friend has a bad man after her and needs her privacy respected."

"No problem." The kid's eyes were like an owl's now as he looked ready to dash about and get everything I had requested, his sleepiness forgotten. "Here's the keys to units six through ten, at the far end of the motel. I'll bring your extra stuff straight away."

"There's a generous tip in it if you stock number ten first."

"Sure. Be right there." The kid turned and hurried into the back through the open doorway while I headed outside to move the Mercedes out of sight. I didn't want anyone to spot it in the off-chance the pair of crooks was still looking for us.

Mira woke up as I slid into the driver's seat, rubbing her eyes. "Sorry, I drifted off. We're here."

I started the vehicle and placed it in drive. "Yes, sleepy head. You know that you snore?" I teased, enjoying the look of indignation that came over her lovely face.

"I do not!" She sat up straighter. "What are you doing?"

"Pulling round back to keep from being seen from the road."

"Good idea." She yawned, managing even to make the simple action look awesome, then stretched her arms over her head, allowing me a perky sideways view of her curvy breasts.

I swallowed, then forced my eyes ahead to finish the task of parking the vehicle safely. "We're in number ten." I jumped out and grabbed her bag while she unbuckled and got to her feet.

"You could get only one room?" she asked, her eyebrows rising.

"Not exactly, but I wanted to keep you safe. I'll sit up and be on watch."

"Oh, but you need to sleep. I can't ask you to do that."

We walked side by side around the motel and met the young boy already unlocking number ten, his arms loaded down.

"Here's the extra stuff." He hurried inside and set everything down on a counter. "I'll stock the others now."

"The others?" Mira asked as the boy rushed past her, clutching the five one-hundred-dollar bills I'd handed him in his fingers.

"With the *no vacancy* sign on, no one else should be stopping by, and that's the best way to keep you safe."

"You think they'll go to that much trouble to find me?" Now she looked so worried I was hit with regret for telling her my plan. "And how rich are you exactly?"

"Let's just say I'm comfortable."

"Only rich people say that. The rest of us spend our lives digging for scraps. Oh sorry, I'm just tired." She rubbed her forehead. "That's not like me, I'm not usually so dark, preferring to see the cup half-filled, you know."

"You need to rest. Too much happened tonight. Go—do what you have to, and I'll keep watch."

"Okay, thanks." She unzipped her overnight bag I'd placed on one of the two beds in the room and pulled out a bag of toiletries and a large, faded T-shirt that had an illustration of a fanciful unicorn imprinted on the front. The childishness of the image hit home and brought with it a realization of just how vulnerable Mira was. And the fact that I was being drawn in deeper and deeper.

I got busy and positioned an armchair near the window. It gave a good view of the road in front of the motel and all the parking spots in front of each unit. Sitting down, I pulled the drapes, leaving just enough of a space open to watch all comings and goings.

The shower started up in the bathroom, leading my mind astray to imagining Mira naked, the water spraying all over her glorious flesh. The image heated my blood and sent most of it to my raging hard-on. *Crap.* How exactly was I supposed to avoid temptation living with a goddess day and night?

Minutes passed in an agonizing slowness while my hearing stayed on high alert. I kept a close watch on the parking lot, though it was doubtful we'd been followed. It was all quiet outside, the only sounds those of nature. Moths beating themselves against light stands and insects chorusing each other in wild abandon. My wolf awoke. The moments before sunrise were when he always demanded release, wanting to come alive and embrace the new day that dawned.

The door to the bathroom creaked open and I could do nothing but turn my head to watch her. Her long bare legs glowing with summer tan, her breasts naked and free swaying under the thin T-shirt all made my mouth water. The floral scent, far stronger now, violets with undernotes of musk raced across the room toward me, stunning and arousing at the same time.

What lunacy was this? I gripped the arms of the chair with my hands, my fingers turning white from the effort I made to restrain myself. My wolf howled and my cock turned to solid iron. The need to bury myself in her hit hard, the urge to mark and bite her hit harder. I could no more close my eyes to the vision that was Mira than I could stop breathing altogether. I had to be with her. *Or die trying.*

"Sorry I used up all the hot water," she said.

"What?" My mind was too focused on other things to make sense of her words.

"The hot water? I didn't realize there was a limit and it turned cold by the time I finished."

"I'm fine." *No, I'm not.* If I stayed in this room a second longer, I was going to leap on her, bury myself in her until we became one.

I gritted my teeth so hard my jaw ached. Holding on to my last bit of sanity, I forced my eyes to close. Now all I could do was smell her arousal. It helped a tiny bit, enough to allow me to control myself.

"I'm going to watch from outside." Staying inside would be torturous, and I could not trust myself. I jumped to my feet and grabbed the armchair, preparing to lug it in front of the motel unit. At least there maybe my cock would stop demanding what it wanted so desperately.

"But you need to rest too." She looked confused as she stood there, innocent and pure.

"I'm fine," I growled and maneuvered the chair through the doorway, setting it in front of the door. *There.* No way anyone was getting past me.

Breathing in the aridness of the high desert, so different from the moist heather-and-moss-tinged air of Castle Creigbourne, stirred an odd emotion for me as I scanned the landscape for any threats. An instant longing for home hit me in the solar plexus.

It was only my cell phone ringing that jerked me away from the odd moment.

Recognizing the number, I groaned. What was I going to report about this eventful and confusing night that would keep my charge in the clear? Mira needed protection more than she needed condemnation. My whole view of her had taken a one-eighty since I was given the case, and now I was invested in the outcome more than I could ever have imagined. But answer I must.

Chapter Ten

Mira

What was Calan doing dragging the furniture out of the motel? There were two perfectly good beds in the room. Not that I would object to sleeping in the same one. He was some man. A man I found myself being more and more drawn to. What would it be like to be with him? He was obviously rich, intelligent, far too good-looking and a protector of women.

Or at least of this woman, making the whole unexpected package truly amazing. And yet somehow our worlds had come together. Was it fate? It sure felt like it. Never before had I wanted a man to jump my bones and have his way with me the first night we met. And I made no excuses for that. Because this would end soon, and I could not live with the regret of not embracing a moment that may never come again.

Decision made, I opened the motel door and adopted my most alluring posture, not that I'd had much practice. "Why don't you come inside and join me? I could really use the company, Calan Creig."

He was talking on his cell phone but gave a hurried, "I'll need to call you back. Something's come up."

We stared at each other across the short distance and his eyes changed. They began to glow greener even as the full moon broke through the clouds, glinting across the parking lot. I had to go to work in a few hours and this opportunity would be lost forever unless I called in sick, which I hesitated to do. I take pride in my job and hated to miss a day. But that led to the worry of what if those criminals found me there?

"Sweetheart, you don't know what you're asking," he warned, speeding my intakes of breaths to double time.

"I'm asking for you and me to be together in the carnal sense. Straightforward enough?"

But the fact he didn't leap to his feet to take me to bed added a certain awkward hesitation.

He shook his head and my spirits dropped. "It's not as simple as that. Much as I want to, you aren't aware of all that's going on right now. It wouldn't be right."

Confused, I couldn't do anything but stare at him. Finally, I found my voice. "What don't I know?"

He looked away then, his expression impossible to read.

I crossed my arms over my chest and leaned against the doorframe. "Please, don't leave me hanging like this. I deserve to know what's going on. Why you don't want to be with me?" Did I totally misread the signals? My confidence faltered at the hit.

He turned back to me. "You must know I want you so much it hurts."

The way he looked at me in that moment, as if he wanted to ravish me on the spot, made me feel like we were the last two people alive. *Undeniable instant lust.* My body overheated from the sensation shooting through me, making it all the more difficult to understand the problem.

"Then what's stopping us? What are you not telling me?"

"I need to stay on guard. We're not that far from your house. You should be resting, and if not, then we need to move on. Find a safer place to hide. Not that I couldn't keep you safe anywhere, but it would ease my mind."

Calan scanned the area, as if he sensed a threat. The way his hands gripped the armchair until his fingers turned white, bloodless, I wasn't certain which threat he was really talking about. Taking me to bed, spilling the beans he was hiding, or those damn idiots on our tail? And all I wanted to do was ease the lust between us, bring it down to a manageable level if that were possible.

Maybe there really was something to this instant attraction in a genetic mating? A number of animals mated for life, the gray wolf instantly coming to mind, and swans. Not that Calan and I were mates and going to spend a lifetime together, but hell, the attraction was certainly there. So why was he fighting it?

"Fine. But I will be going to work in a few hours," I said stiffly when nothing more was forthcoming and shut the door behind myself with a little more force than strictly necessary.

The door slammed open no sooner than I had taken two steps and Calan stood in the doorway. "You can't go to work. Those men will know where you work. I forbid it."

"You forbid it!" He might as well have thrown the green flag at a sporting event. I wanted to pounce on him then, make him take those dire words back. And here I thought he was a champion of women.

I poked him in the chest with one finger, surprised at how solid and firm it was as my finger bounced off. I still wanted him which annoyed me even further. "You don't get to say that to me, ever! You understand? I'm my own woman. No one forbids me from doing whatever it is I want to."

"Even if it means putting yourself in danger?" His eyes glinted dangerously in the dim light of the motel room.

Heat flashed through me, the toxic heat of anger and pent-up passion. My last nerve shattered. "This town has cops, for heaven's sake! I can dial nine-one-one if need be."

"Before those gangsters whisk you away to God knows where to do God knows what to you? No, you need to reconsider your new situation. Those men—they're serious. I only spoke for your own good, to get your attention."

He changed his tone, now trying to be the voice of reason. I was *not* going to let him forget anytime soon how profoundly angry his forbidding me had made me, but I needed to know more.

"Now that you have it, mind telling me what's going on? You said there's a reason we can't be together." I backed away from him, from the annoying temptation that still fired my blood, and sat down on the edge of the bed. He looked pained at first, then nodded.

"Earlier tonight, when I said that while I was burying the goods and was hurt by a shovel accident…that's not what happened."

"Go on." Mystified, I could only stare at him before I bit my lip and turned away. Far too much distraction. Like looking at the sun. I expected my retinas to be burned to a crisp.

"That Tasmanian you're looking to report on, he showed up. Challenged me to a fight."

"What? Why would he do that? And why couldn't you tell me that?"

"I didn't want to frighten you any more than you already were. I think he's stalking you. I discovered him skulking through the back fence."

"He attacked you? I'm truly sorry about that. But did he say anything? Did you see him as a wolf and as a man?" My anger forgotten for the moment, I pounced on Calan's words.

"Wolf. He had that unusual striping on his back common to the Tasmanian."

"But this is good. It means contact. If I go back home, he might appear again and I can film him. Make a record that might hold up in proper channels."

"What?" Calan shook his head, obviously wanting to forbid me or something equally annoying, but he was working hard to supress the words—I'll give him that—at least judging by the strained expression on his face. And he had my back tonight, even if he'd hit one sour note. I couldn't stay mad forever at the guy who was trying to help me.

"Why not? He has no reason to harm me, right? He's in hiding, probably afraid of exposure."

"He's dangerous, Mira. He attacked me. I had to fight him off. It was only a police siren that halted it, before he turned tail and ran."

"He clawed you? That's what those marks were." I didn't like that Calan had been hurt on my account. I had to remember that he had been dragged into this, not of his volition, but because he was protecting me. I did need to cut him some slack.

"It was nothing. I'm fine. But he might be seeing you as a conquest. He's a dangerous, unknown entity. You can't expect me to be fine with you returning to your house. And don't forget those men who are after you for a whole other reason." Calan shook his head. "This is a crazy situation. My best advice is you need to get somewhere very safe for a while. Take a few days off work. Figure things out. I'll book a suite at any one of the fine hotels you'd like to stay at. We can hole up in relative comfort and security. How about it?"

I still had the feeling that he was holding something back from me. But what could it be? *Maybe a girlfriend or a wife?*

"You're not married or in a serious relationship, are you?" I was a bit late in asking, but he was hiding something.

He snorted. "No. Definitely not."

He said it with such derision that it took my attention away from other things.

"Why do you find the idea so abhorrent?" I asked, a bit stiffly. I mean, what's so bad about having a girlfriend? Women can be besties.

"My job—no way would I submit a woman to the risk of losing her mate and dying alone."

"That's a bit dramatic, don't you think?"

He shook his head, his expression closed to discussion, like he'd already said too much.

I made an instant decision. "I'm calling my friend Amy. She'll take me in."

"That's not in your best interests." The grim line of his mouth backed up his dire words.

"What do you know about it? You showed up yesterday, and sure, I'm grateful for your help and always will be, but I'm a big girl. I can take care of myself. Amy's a good friend. She'll have my back just like I've had hers."

I'd known Amy Stratton since university. Sure, we competed at times for the same jobs, but I could count on her, just as she could count on me. I had no idea why I hadn't thought of calling her earlier. *Blame it on my hormones and the situation that scrambled my brains.*

Before he could object further, I brought up Amy's cell number. I hated to wake her in the middle of the night, but it couldn't be helped. I needed to bail on my current situation. Let Mr. McHottie or Rambo, or whoever he thought he was, return to his life.

"Besides, don't you have an aunt and uncle to help move? Tourist attractions to take in?" I asked pointedly and moved as far away as the motel room allowed to speak with my friend.

The phone rang more times than I was comfortable with. Finally, a sleepy voice came on the line.

"Hey, Mira. What's up, girl?"

"Can I stay with you? Somethings come up and I need a place to stay."

"Sure. I thought you might me calling about something I did earlier tonight." Amy cleared her throat. "I'm sorry, I was drinking and I…I don't know, I made a mess of things. But it's not like anyone's going to believe it, right? But of course you can stay with me. No need to ask. That's if you still want to after you, well, see it."

"What are you talking about?" Mystified, I gripped the phone tighter, a ball of unease growing in the pit of my stomach.

"So you didn't see the post yet. God, I'm really sorry. I should have warned you first. Check Facebook, okay? Then we can talk when you get here. I gotta a big box of wine with your name on it. We can call in sick and spend the day together, if you'd like?" Amy sounded desperate now and that only heightened my dread.

"Okay. Let me just see what's going on."

I hung up and with trembling fingers brought up my Facebook account, dreading and knowing something bad had happened, that a ship had sailed that could not be brought back to shore. And there it was on Amy's home page. My video of the Tasmanian posted as Amy Stratton's own original work. My best friend had betrayed me. Left me to hang in the wind.

"*Oh no*. Why would she do that, drunk or not? This is bad." I sank down onto the nearest bed, all the energy in my body instantly gone. My throat thickened with unshed tears. *Betrayal.* It hurt worse than anything else I had experienced to date. Worse than finding out about Deadbeat, worse than my brother deserting me, worse than having a bunch of drug dealers out for my blood. Amy and I had made a pact. We'd chosen each other to be friends over everyone else. Now she had broken it. Destroyed our friendship over wanting to claim a video as her own. She wanted to become known in the cryptozoology community, same as me. I just never knew she'd knock me down and stamp all over me to do it.

Tears began to flow, dripping down my face to dampen my top. I was just too tired, too exhausted to take the news well, though I hated appearing weak.

Suddenly strong arms were around me, pulling me close. I leaned my face against Calan's broad chest and gave in to my grief.

He patted my back like I was a child, making soothing sounds I could not have imagined the big alpha man ever making, reassuring noises that spoke of kindness and caring as he rocked me gently in his arms. After long moments of feeling a connection to him that defied reason other than he seemed to be absorbing a lot of my mourning and keening, I felt a bit better, able to at least face my new reality.

Calan dried my face with his shirt tail when I finally pulled away from him.

"What was all that about?" he asked gently.

"Horrible stuff I don't want to talk about, okay? Let's just say I won't be going over to my friend's house anytime soon. God, I must look a sight."

"You look beautiful. How could you not, sweetheart?"

His words blessed me with a new calmness. A new awareness of how close we were together, his hot body touching mine. How wonderful it felt, and how much I wanted it to continue.

"Kiss me, please," I said, needing nothing more in the whole world at that moment than to be with Calan, to feel him inside me, taking me away from all this.

He brought up his hands to cup my face, crushing his mouth to mine. Something unleashed between us. Something so powerful that nothing except the end of the world could have stopped it.

The kiss was raw. *So raw.* It spoke of passion and pain and fury. He forced his tongue between my lips and took, just took. My whole body quivered. *Oh. My. God.* I was lost. I wanted to give him all I had. *And take as much back.*

He devoured me and I melted against him, letting him in and releasing the pain. I needed this as much as him, maybe more. To feel something other than grief and pain and loss.

He thrust his tongue into my mouth. *Plundered it.* He tasted so good, the lingering whiskey from earlier melding with his warm cinnamon breath. He grabbed the back of my hair, his fingers tugging apart the neat braid I'd put back in for bed and the long lengths flowing around us like a curtain. Electric jolts arrowed straight to my pussy. No man had grabbed me like that. *Ever.* As if we were the last two people and he wanted me more than life itself. He pulled off his shirt, and I admired his physique in a mind fog, dimly aware of the corded muscles of steel that gripped me.

I returned his kiss with greed. *Hot. Searing. Greed.* My arousal dampened my panties. I breathed in the fragrance of sex filtering into the air, the mingling of male and female essence arousing as hell, stirring my senses into a blazing passion of white light. Blood roared in my ears, an insistent drumbeat mimicking a heartrate.

He ripped his mouth from mine, sucking on my neck, trailing tiny kisses down toward my breasts. I wanted him to go farther. Much farther. He pressed into me, caressing my shoulders, then coming around to fondle my breasts, using his fingers to roll the tender budded nipples. With my body about to give way and fall back on the bed, he steadied me, sucking on one nipple then the other through the fabric of my shirt and bra. I arched my body to give him full access, my mind screaming, *take me, take me now. Help me forget.*

Fire and ice. Hot passion melted my body into a quicksilver pool of both, swirling one sensation against the other, tugging me into a growing vortex. It near drowned me, pulling me under, unable to see past my need. To have him drive that huge, thick cock grinding against my pussy inside me now that we'd fallen to the bed, dissolving into pure lust.

"Talk dirty to me. Tell me what you want," I whispered. *Anything to take my mind away.* This was all new for me and I wanted it that way, something unlike ever before to experience. His breath scorched my skin where the kisses landed, his beard that had been growing overnight lightly scratching my sensitive flesh. It drove me wild. He pulled off my shirt with hands made golden by the sun, throwing it aside. Under my searching fingers, his flesh corded and bulged with solid muscles.

"I want to fuck you, fuck you until you're screaming for mercy. And I won't stop, not until you can't remember who you are. I'm going to fuck you, fuck you raw." He punctuated each word with a kiss on my flesh, his lips insistent.

He pushed my thighs wide apart, rubbing me through the cloth of my pants, his touch causing my clit to ache and swell as my pussy lips opened farther. He could feel my heat, the dampness through the fabric. I pushed against his pressing fingers. I wanted to be naked under him, have him press that wall of flesh against mine, fuck me senseless. *Make me forget.*

"Yes, oh yes. I want you to fuck me. I *need* you to fuck me."

Calan's cell phone rang.

I froze, opening my eyes to see his frustration at being interrupted obvious in the heavy frown that clouded his expression. I swallowed hard.

He hesitated another second, then pulled away, leaving me irritated and bereft of his passion. What in the hell was I thinking?

He opened his pocket and took out his phone…then switched it off and threw it aside.

Calan leaned down and kissed me gently on the lips. He pressed his forehead to mine for a moment before letting me go, taking on a mantle of determination, like a man ready to do battle for me. The gesture touched my heart.

He reached out to steady me. I looked into his eyes, touched his face with trembling fingers. I caressed the smooth planes of his skin. He moved, gliding his lips over my palm, kissing it. My body was needy and insistent. He sucked one of my fingers into his mouth, his eyes locking with mine.

A low moan escaped as he bent and kissed me, crushing me to his broad chest. He caressed my back, clamped his mouth to mine, seeking my tongue, searching, tantalizing, reaching for something more. My body trembled under the onslaught as I slid my hands across the hard-roped muscles of his forearms, relishing the smooth bronzed skin decorated with ancient tribal tattoos. A drumbeat started again in my blood, drowning out the world.

The pants I wore were confining, annoying, keeping me from experiencing naked flesh against mine.

He cupped my breasts, thumbing the pebbled nipples. An intolerable throbbing began, my pussy clenching with need. My breath caught in my throat as he yanked my jeans and underwear off, baring my naked body to his view. He sucked on one nipple, then the other, making me whimper. God, I want his fingers stroking me, his cock stretching me, bringing me to completion.

I grabbed his hand and brought it to my mound. He groaned, his fingers pressing against my swollen, slick and wet pussy, nudging the outer lips apart, searching for my clit. I opened my legs wide, wanting him.

"Fuck me, Calan. Now."

"Mira." He pulled away, took my face in his hands and made me look up at him. "I don't want to take advantage of you, no matter how much I want you. I can't do that." His cock pressing hard into my belly through the fabric of his dress pants, showed how very much it would cost him if we didn't continue. He shook his head. "I can't do that."

"I want you, Calan. Don't make me beg. I need this more than you can know. I have to have you inside me. Please, please don't stop now. Take me, fill me. Make me yours. Make me forget, if just for one night."

My pussy pulsed, the walls contracting, demanding fulfillment. He caressed my cheek as if searching for the truth in my upturned face. I saw the moment he came to a decision, making my breath hitch and my pussy clench tighter. His eyes darkened. Naked, I watched him stand up and begin to tear off his clothes.

"I'm going to fuck you every way possible, Mira, all night long, until you can't take it anymore," he promised, a low-pitched thrumming resonating in his tone. His boxers slid down his muscled thighs.

I swallowed hard. The musty odor of sex permeated the motel room. "Good. I want that. I want you, all of you."

He stood naked and proud, his huge cock jutting upward, the immense size making my eye widen farther.

I reached out for him, beckoning him to the bed. "Come here."

He strode forward and pushed my knees upward and out, positioning himself between my thighs.

"I'm going to taste you. God, your scent, like violets and sugar." He slipped his fingers between my thighs, touching my pussy, pulling the lips apart, then swept his tongue down my channel.

I shuddered, coming right off the bed, pleasure rolling in tight waves, making me throb with an acute need for release. He teased me, using his thumb to lightly circle my clit, pushing a thick finger inside me, then adding a second one that made me moan aloud and thrash my head back and forth, caught in a whirlwind of sensations.

"You taste like honey," he growled, my essence glistening on his lips. "But I need to be inside you." He rubbed his lips with the back of his hand. "I'll get a condom."

He got up, making me mewl. I was so lost in the desert that I didn't care. He grabbed his pants and pulled out a condom, tearing the package open, then rolling the latex sheath over his cock.

"Hurry," I urged him.

The intense look on his face warmed something deep inside me, something that had never been alive. It sizzled to life as the power of his gaze spread throughout my body.

He came to me then, stared down at me as I lay there, welcoming him. "You are so beautiful, open to me like that. Christ, you make me so hard, woman." He grabbed his cock as if to emphasize his words. A warrior stood before me, an ancient warrior that would rock my world. I melted into a puddle of want and lust.

"Fuck me now like this is our only time to be together."

The stark words hung between us for an instant, piercing, vibrating, making me aware of the life-or-death stakes hanging over us with so many looking to do me harm. He fell on me hungrily after that slight moment of realization, of hesitation, as if there were no tomorrow—for there might very well not be for us. He used his fingers to separate my labia, thrusting his cock into me without preamble. I was beyond ready, opening to him, more than I had imagined possible. His deep thrusts pushed me to the edge, make the drive for release almost painful in its intensity. The pleasure-pain drove me onward, searching, searching, yearning…

"Yes! Fuck me—just like that. Hard! Harder!" I gripped his ass with my fingers, my legs spread wide as he pumped his cock into me. "God, yes. Don't stop."

He obliged my entreaties, continuing for long precious moments, sweat dripping, unimaginable heat coursing through me. The wild sounds of flesh slapping against flesh, salty and alive. *Alive.* The word seared my brain and drove me to new heights. I pushed against him, lost in the sensation of powerful, mind-blowing sex. Over and over again.

"I can't hold off any longer," he warned. "Come for me, sweetheart. I need you to come for me."

My mind absorbed his words, allowing me to finally fall over the edge. I set herself free at that moment, slipped away from earthly bonds, away from anything but being in the moment.

His body jerked a few times, his hips bucking against mine. We lay back, exhausted, breathing heavily.

"That was un-fucking-believable," he murmured, his eyes glowing as he stared down at me. He moved away and pulled off the condom before throwing it into the trash, then turning on his side to draw me close.

"It was," I agreed. My lips curled upward into a smile

"I like that," he said. He traced my mouth with a finger.

"What?"

"That smile. You need to smile more often."

I stared into his eyes, seeing my own reflection hovering over his soul in the greenest depths. "Nice to have something to smile about."

"You need to be fucked, and often."

"I won't disagree with that assessment." I trailed my fingers down his chest, the smooth skin warm and firm under my fingertips. "But I can see you need it just as badly." He was already hard, his cock rising between his muscled thighs.

"Good thing we've got all night." An unspoken agreement between them to stay in the moment simmered under the surface, freeing me to be myself, to reach out to him with all I possessed. He grasped my breast, circling my hardening nipple with a thumb and forefinger, gently tugging on it. His actions sent tingles of pleasure to my pussy. Arousing me. *How can I still need more of this man?* It defied reason. But there it was. My channel clenched anew.

"Good thing." I reached up and stroked his cheek. "My turn to pleasure you."

"Let me wash up first," he said, slipping out of bed. He was back. Fast.

I got onto my knees and tugged him to the bed with an outstretched hand, positioning myself between his thighs. I gave him a half-smile, grasped him at the base of his cock, then preceded to lick and kiss and suck my way down the thick shaft and over his balls, his deep groans of pleasure all the thanks I needed.

Chapter Eleven

Calan

I swept Mira's strawberry-colored locks back from her face, watching her lick and kiss and suck her way down my shaft and over my balls, then back up again. An indescribable sensation took hold of me. Centering in my balls, the heat surged up from underneath, and the more she caressed me, the hotter it became.

"So fucking good. That's it," I said, fisting her hair, my balls and cock beginning to throb in undulating waves, giving over to a heavenly release. Her throat worked to swallow it all and I immediately wanted her again. Never had I been so in tune with a woman in bed. Never had I wanted to fuck a woman over and over again until she was completely mine. She was so ready and wet and willing. It scared me, far worse than anything else ever had. To find a woman accepting me for who I was at that moment, to feel such intensity vibrating in her tiny body as she took my cock inside her without question—it was beyond amazing. Maybe this kind of intensity would burn itself out by morning. Or maybe not...

"I don't know if I can ever let you get out of this bed," I teased and tucked a curl behind her ear, my heart and mind filled with worry that this amazing time would end. That something would come along and drive us apart. No, I couldn't allow that. No matter what happened, there had to be a way for us to be together. No way could I give up this woman anytime soon.

She placed her fingertips to my lips, hushing me. "What matters is now. Not what may or may not be in the future. Don't they always say enjoy the now, that the present is all we have?"

I swallowed hard and pulled her roughly to me. If this was all we had, I was going to make damn sure every second counted. Because right now, I could feel the universe closing in on us. Secrets kept are dynamite. And I had more than my fair share—keeping from Mira what I was, and what I knew.

"What got you so upset earlier?" I finally thought to ask, now that the haze of passion had been satiated enough to bear reason.

"Do we have to talk about it? Okay, I don't want secrets between us. That's the surest way to end things when they blow up in your face, right?"

Her words sent a shard of worry straight to my belly, tightening it uncomfortably.

"Go on," I encouraged her.

"It's what Amy did earlier tonight. Said she was drunk when she posted that video I made on Facebook as if it were her own. Not sure I believe her. It hurt to think she'd do that to me—to our friendship. Still does."

The damning words made me scramble to find my cell phone. *Shit.* Cristaldo had called again. And now I knew why. Mira's friend Amy had just unleashed a firestorm on all our heads. There was no time to wonder how a so-called friend could do that. Now I had to go into damage control. *Immediately.* Figure out a way through the minefield that was blowing up around us.

The sound of something on the roof above our motel room took my full attention. *Damn it!* I should have been on guard. A dereliction of my duty. Now all hell was about to break loose.

"What is that? What's going on?" Mira asked, her expression wide-eyed and a touch fearful.

I kissed Mira, trying to calm her. "Don't move from this bed. I'll take care of this and be right back. Everything's going to be fine."

"But—"

More sounds of scratching and scrambling around on the motel's low roof interrupted whatever it was she was going to say. She pulled the sheet up around her neck as I leapt from the bed. There had to be at least two idiots sneaking about up there, and they were gunning for me. Did the Tasmanian have pack members, and if so, how many? Things had taken an unforeseen twist, one that had backed me into a corner.

I turned back to Mira. I had no other choice than to warn her, something that could tear our fragile beginning to shreds. "No matter what happens in the next few minutes, know that this meant something to me." I gestured between us. "And I want it to continue."

"What do you mean? What's going to happen?"

There was no point in getting dressed. With two creeps after me, I would need to shift to wolf to protect her.

"I'm locking the door. Don't let anybody in but me. Okay?" I asked when she didn't answer me. Maybe I could pull this off, keep her from seeing the fight that had to happen. I quickly texted my Vegas contact in the WSL and told him to bring reinforcements, but to hold off and watch from a short distance. I hadn't done it earlier as I didn't want any undue attention on Mira, but now it couldn't be helped.

God forbid but if the unexpected happened, I needed to know that she would be protected. If I could go this alone, I would, though. Otherwise, Mira would discover a secret that could bust our lives wide open and stop any chance of us moving forward. I ignored the ramifications of this new idea born of our mating this night, of wanting to be with her in the future, and focused on what had to be done now.

"Aren't you going to get dressed?"

"No time. And what scares away an intruder quicker than a having a wild naked Scotsman confronting them, right?" I made fun of it, hoping she'd buy it.

"Maybe if one naked person is helpful, two would be even more effective?" she asked, her eyes alight with a touch of humor.

I might have fallen a bit in love with her at that moment, with her feistiness, seeing her following my lead. Our eyes locked and I could see the trust in hers clear as day. *Oh God, please don't let those damn Tasmanians destroy everything.*

"Stay put and out of sight," I warned, and, hearing the noises escalate overhead, kissed her once more and rushed from the room, closing the door firmly behind me.

The sunrise still not in evidence and no pedestrians in view, I quickly shifted to wolf. Howling my displeasure at the night skies, I leapt onto the roof and confronted the Tasmanians. There were two of them stomping around, both in wolf form, and both turned to glare at me, eyes gleaming red in the moonlight. One rushed me, the one I had fought with earlier, while the other roof rat circled around to try to ambush me from behind. No hiding from me—I would take both of these assholes down and anyone else that tried to come between me and Mira. *No one gets between a wolf and his mate. No one.*

I let the first wolf come straight at me, then, at the last second, I leapt to the side, spun halfway around, and slammed him with a glancing blow to his right side. He whined a high-pitched squeal in answer to the rush of pain, skidding to a stop at the edge of the roof just in time to avoid plunging to the ground.

The second wolf lost no time in charging me, grasping for my throat, then spinning away as I bared my teeth to nip at his back haunch. My teeth took out a chunk of flesh that I spit onto the rooftop. The pair, learning the lesson of my prowess, lowered themselves closer to the roof to protect their vulnerable bellies, skulking around me, looking for an opening.

Working together now, one came at me from behind while the other circled around back. Suddenly, both attacked at the same time. Ass over tea kettle, the three of us spun in a blur of movement, limbs flaying and teeth gashing, dangerous movements that could throw anyone of us off the edge with a broken neck at any second. One caught me with his teeth on my foreleg and I ignored the pain, while I crunched down on the back of the neck of the other and didn't let go, sinking my fangs into his vulnerable spine.

A screech of instant pain before the body went limp. Bloodlust filled me as I felt the intruder's life end. I fought, for Mira, for us, for the future. Throwing the limp body aside, I spun to confront the second wolf. He was more cautious now, afraid to end up the same as his partner in crime. His red eyes bore into mine, ripe with indecision. Then he turned and leapt from the roof and from view. I ventured to the side he'd disappeared from and saw how he'd managed it. A shed perched a few feet below allowed him easy access to escape. He ran across the open field behind the motel, vanishing into the desert.

The dead wolf, eyes glazing over, stared up at me. He'd died as wolf, he'd be buried as wolf. I picked up the carcass and adjusted the weight. I needed to hide it before sunrise. I eased the body down the back of the motel onto the shed, grunting at the pain that it created for my open wounds that dripped blood in a steady flow to darken the dirt below. There was no time to heal by staying in my wolf form for long—even now false dawn was beginning to turn the dark skies to charcoal-gray streaks. Soon the world would be waking up and my actions might be seen.

I leapt to the ground. Then shifting to man, I hauled the body up over my shoulders, fireman-style, and began to pace across the open ground to the treeline. In short order I vanished into the Joshua trees, looking for a place to stash the body until I could come back with a shovel. My luck held, and I found a good resting spot, a small cave that went far enough back to hide the body in. Placing it inside, I said a short prayer for his mortal soul, then began the hike back to the motel, annoyed by my obvious limp. The damn bastard had damaged another tendon, by the feel of it. I kept a sharp eye out for company and caught the sweet fragrance of Mira before I spotted her.

She stood at the back of the motel, dressed now and looked worried and upset, holding a fire extinguisher she'd pried off the wall like she intended to use it as a weapon. *Christ.* Had she seen anything? How long had she been standing there?

I straightened up best I could and approached her, hating that she'd seen me damaged by the fight. I had a sudden worry that there might be more of the Tasmanians lurking in the desert, that a small pack might exist, one that had been hiding and growing for decades, only now coming to light.

"You took down a wolf with your bare hands. How is that even possible?" she accused me.

"Why didn't you stay put like I asked? What did you see?" I asked, knowing it wasn't good. I wanted to take her in my arms, but I stank of the fight and was covered in blood.

"I couldn't let you fight two of them by yourself, so I grabbed this and came out to help you. I saw you carry a wolf over your shoulders out that way." She nodded at the treeline. "What's going on? You owe me an explanation, Calan Creig or whoever you are. And was the one you killed the Tasmanian I videoed?"

"Perhaps we could go inside. I need a shower and a drink. Then I'll tell you everything you need to know."

"*Everything.* No holding back, Calan. We clear? Otherwise, I'm calling an Uber and taking my chances on my own."

"Fine."

We slipped back into the motel room, a few feet and an ocean between us, just as the first rays of sunlight began racing across the landscape, preparing to bring the day.

Without another word, I hurried to shower, disgusted at having my body fouled by the Tasmanians. But as the hot water swirled the dirt and blood down the drain, worries loomed. How to explain this to Mira? Because I knew without a doubt that she was my fated mate, the one called Forever Mate by our clan. The one I had never expected to find, and the one that could bring me to my knees if I wasn't careful.

I slicked back my long hair and tied a towel around my waist. Time for the moment of truth. Or at least as little as I could get away with and still keep her bound to my side.

"Okay. What is it you want to know?" I asked, exiting the bathroom to find her sitting on the armchair like a queen in a throne room.

"How does a mortal man, even as big and strong as you look"— she swallowed, then continued—"kill a wolf with your bare hands?"

I shrugged. "I got lucky."

She snorted. "Not going to cut it. Unless you have some magical powers I haven't seen yet?"

"What, my magical powers in bed didn't sway you?"

"Fine. Was the wolf striped? A Tasmanian?"

I nodded. "Unfortunately, yes. The second one got away."

"The other was also Tasmanian?" Her anger forgotten for a second, her eyes widened with interest. "Two Tasmanians. There may be more?"

"I hope not." I slammed the door on liking that possibility.

"But this is important! It proves my case that the Tasmanian wolf is back. Did you see it shift to human form?"

I shook my head—thankful she hadn't seen me shift either. "No sign of that."

"I want to go and see its body. I need to have it transported to the lab at the zoo. This must be investigated."

"No, let it lie, Mira."

"What! This is an amazing opportunity. I can't *not* do this. You're free to go. I got this now."

Now she was forcing my hand, damn it. She had no idea what she was asking. What exposure could bring. I needed to appeal to her common sense, override this need for her to create a name for herself.

"Have you forgotten about those guys after you? You go to work and you're a sitting target."

"I can handle a bunch of drug dealers. What are they going to do, really? The police can take care of them if they have the audacity to show up at my workplace."

Fuck. Nothing was working. I rubbed the back of my neck in frustration. "Okay, you leave me no choice. You're walking into a minefield if you continue to expose the werewolf part of the equation. Stick with the animal being of an extinct species and drop that part."

"Why should I? It's an amazing discovery. Too late now anyway with Amy posting it to Facebook as her own," Mira reminded me.

I thought frantically of what to do. My mind had been too occupied by my cock this night to think straight. "She must take it down. Immediately!"

"Doubtful. She's getting all the attention she craves. I still can't believe she'd do that to me. Choosing fame over friendship." Mira's eyes filled with tears that she dashed away with the back of her hand. She had a strange look on her face, like she realized how much she also wanted her work to matter, but was uncertain of what line she would cross to achieve her goals. "Maybe I see myself a little too well. But I'd *never* stab a friend in the back, though I might beg for help if my house gets trashed by those assholes after me."

"Mira, this is no joke. Oh God, now I need to tell you everything."

"That's what I've been trying to tell you!"

"You're not going to like it. Maybe it's best I just show you, though I do have some good news to share as well." What other choice did I have? I couldn't protect a woman who didn't realize the monumental danger she was in. Those drug dealers that I had neutralized were nothing compared to the ire of a werewolf pack worrying about exposure.

"First off, the good news—you can quit worrying about those drug dealers coming after you ever again."

"What do you mean?"

"I had them paid off last night by one of my employees. They'll be leaving you and your brother alone from now on."

"What? I don't understand." She gave me a look of amazement, her eyes blinking with disbelief.

"I'm rich." I shrugged. "Why not help you in any way I can? So at least now you can know your house won't be trashed or that they'll show up at work to bother you."

She shook her head before comprehension dawned. "Why didn't you tell me last night? You led me to believe I was in danger from them."

"Maybe because I wanted to spend time getting to know you. If you could have just gone home again, then you wouldn't need me."

"That's kind of sweet." She blushed, arousing my protective instincts. "I'll pay you back, whatever it takes. I promise."

"No need."

"I pay my debts, Calan." Her tone was sterner now. "Now, what's the bad news?"

"It's not really bad, *per se*."

"Quite hedging. Much as I appreciate your looking after my interests, and spending time with you—" She glanced at the messy bed with another charming blush.

Her fresh arousal at being reminded of her night's lovemaking scented the air, drawing me up by my bootstraps. *We should be mating, not worrying about this shit,* my inner wolf chimed in.

"I need to know everything, Calan. You can't build a friendship on lies and secrets. It never works."

"This part is a harder to explain. It's not like you don't understand cryptozoology, right? Just promise me you won't be frightened. I would never hurt you, Mira. You need to know that."

Her expression changed, growing solemn. "You're not one of them, right? You can't be, you're of Scots heritage. The original Tasmanians are of Australian heritage."

"No, I'm not Tasmanian. I'm a Wulver, entirely different."

Her beautiful eyes were now rounded and vague, like she was barely holding on to reality. Even her voice sounded strange, breathless and whispery. Had she been through too much in the past twelve hours to manage another startling revelation? But I couldn't stop now, she needed to know so I could whisk her away to safety, soon as I had dealt with that Amy Stratton character.

"Wulver? The fabled warriors from the Highlands? But why…why are you here now with me?"

"I'm here to warn you. Protect you." And with that I called upon my wolf. A shimmer of light sparked around the portal to the supernatural dimension as it opened up. I flashed through it, my body enduring the change, my cells transforming then aligning in another form to emerge a Wulver.

I was back in the present moment as a huge wolf with a golden coat. The world around me had mutated to colors and tones I could not see as human. Mira's scent was even more powerful in my wolf state, my olfactory nerves sharpened by her arousal. I growled with excitement, overcome by her, just before she slumped to the ground in a dead faint.

Chapter Twelve

Mira

I came to aware of a strange vibration surrounding me. *Where am I?* I sat up, groggy and disorientated, my mouth dry. I must have been sleeping for hours. I blinked, uncertain at first of what I was staring at. I lay on a very comfortable bed, with a curtain for privacy pulled around me, making the space small, like in a hospital emergency room.

When I yanked the drape open, the cabin of a private aircraft greeted my disbelieving eyes. A very sumptuous aircraft with a strange man seated on one of the soft leather seats. He turned and noticed me, his expression calm and respectful. He looked more British than the British, his attire impeccable. Perfect black suit and paisley ascot with a striking stickpin bearing a lustrous pearl anyone would covet.

When he spoke his upper crust accent confirmed my suspicions. "Ah, Miss Tala. Welcome aboard. Alistair at your service. Whatever you need, just ask."

"I need you to turn this plane around and head right back to Vegas."

"I am sorry, that's the one thing I can't do. I enjoy my position with the Creig clan far too much and intend to keep it."

"Why am I here anyway?" A little awed by the man, I didn't erupt into a fit of anger that seemed my right since I had no idea what the hell was going on. Instead, I decided to take the high road, at least for now.

"Calan Creig, an acquaintance and close friend of yours, I believe, has asked me to see to your needs. It appears you were in danger and he squirreled you away for your own safety. We are now headed for Castle Creigbourne in the Highlands where the Creig is looking forward to meeting you."

"And where is Calan?" No one else was in view, though I hoped either Calan was piloting the plane or someone else reliable. My mind was working on remembering events from the night before but was coming up blank as to why I was in this predicament. Last thing I remembered was... *Holy shit!* He'd turned into a wolf! A Wulver. The memory made my head hurt and I swallowed. I couldn't allow myself to see past that point for a moment or I risked freaking out.

"He's attending to another matter and will be joining us as soon as possible at Castle Creigbourne."

"Good." Then I could give him a proper piece of my mind. Because I just realized, *damn it*, if he was a wolf, then he'd known all about who I was before he arrived. It had been a set up from the first moment we'd met. Red-hot anger erupted, making me hang on by a thread to the volcano that threatened to explode all over the man who sat so calmly before me.

It was not Alistair's fault his employer was a goddammed con artist, and a werewolf to boot. Had our lovemaking been fake too? We might have just met, but I thought the attraction was mutual, instinctive, not a way for him to control me. Regret filled me. And damn it, why did we have to be such a perfect match in the bedroom. *Blatantly unfair!*

"I require the use of the ladies' facilities," I stated with as much decorum as I could manage, caught as I was in a state of intense emotion. Alistair's affect was so great that I was finding myself talking similarly to him to cover up the true state of things. It would be funny, if my present predicament was not so disconcerting.

"Of course. It's located closer to the front of the aircraft, through that doorway." Alistair pointed it out.

I stood and my head swam from the suddenness of the movement. Too many thoughts and images pressed in and I forced them away with some difficulty. I shuffled down the short aisle of the aircraft, passed by the man who had to be Mr. McStuffy if Calan was Mr. McHottie, something I would need to consider downgrading. Maybe Mr. Pain-in-my-ass? Or Mr. Go-away-before-I-chew-you-a-new-one? Hurriedly I locked myself in the bathroom which was bigger than expected with a vanity and a shower stall.

Thankful to be alone at last, I stared into the mirror, to see if the unsettling experience was obvious in my face. No, my bright blonde hair was still intact if somewhat disheveled from sleep, my blue eyes still blue, the small scar still visible above my right eyebrow from a tumble off my bicycle while learning to ride it as a kid. I splashed cold water on my face and dried my skin with a thick embossed hand towel that had an embroidered stylized C. *Rich. Right! Rich as sin by the look of it.*

I sat on the stool in front of the vanity and rummaged around in the drawers, finding a hairbrush to make myself more presentable. I couldn't face Mr. McStuffy without making some attempt, however feeble, to improve myself. I would have loved a shower, but I couldn't imagine removing my clothes in such an environment. That would have to wait until I had my bearings.

A few minutes later, face washed and hair in a neat braid, feeling more composed and better prepared to question Mr. McStuffy, I exited the bathroom.

"We are about to land, miss. It would be best for you to buckle yourself in."

Stymied by the timing, I did as he asked, then buttoned my lip. If not Alistair, then the next person to question would be this person called, what was it, yes, *the Creig*. His grandmother sounded like someone with control issues. Probably where Calan got his balls. The guy was insufferable, putting me on an aircraft bound for his homeland.

I stopped myself from snorting in the most unladylike manner under the watchful eye of my host and stared out through the window. The air was misty, but I could make out the outline of a huge castle. Ancient in appearance, its haunting splendor permeated my consciousness. *WOW*. Imagine living in such a place and growing up in its shadow. *Compare that to my own nomadic childhood of double-wides and cheap rental joints.* I shook my head. The Creig clan had it good. Well, now I would make them accountable for my abduction, because a spade was a spade, well meaning or not. I mean, who in their right mind sent someone he'd just met across the open ocean to a foreign country?

I hurried off the plane and toward the imposing castle that dominated the skyline. *Who has their own runway, for heaven's sake?* Intent on finding someone that had a spark of common sense in them, I zeroed in on the entrance and made a beeline for it. Or someone to point me in the way of the nearest airport. I had to get home. I had a job and animals that were my responsibility and required attention.

Alistair brought up the rear, followed by a younger man carrying the bag I'd taken to the motel. Maybe I could beg a shower and fresh clothes? It was another long plane journey back, and I didn't want to be offending my fellow passengers in coach, because there was no way I could afford to go first class.

The door I was approaching flew open just as I reached it. An elderly woman with the look of steely iron in her eyes stood in my path, even her thick white hair vibrating with surplus energy. She gave me a once-over, blocking the way inside. Maybe I was expected to curtsey? She didn't look very impressed with the sight of me. I wasn't either now that I thought about it, all wrinkled and smelly such as I was. Well, it wasn't my fault. I was so nervous I spoke first.

"Hello, ma'am. I'm afraid there's been some kind of misunderstanding. I seem to have landed on your doorstep by mistake—"

"It's no mistake," she said, cutting me off at the knees. "Ye'd better come inside." She then turned like an imperial queen and led the way.

O–kay.

I stepped over the threshold with some obvious trepidation. I mean, the woman could be a clansperson which meant she could be a werewolf. I swallowed my unease and took a deep cleansing breath.

"I was hoping to speak with The Creig?" I spoke a bit louder as I struggled to follow the woman through the twist and turns of the hallway. She was in extremely good shape for a woman who had to be ninety if she were a day. I mean, she was very wrinkled.

She ignored my question or maybe she was hard of hearing? But finally, she slowed down and entered an open doorway. I took in the room as I hurried through it. A library filled with shelves and shelves of books. It had a bit of a musty odor that was not unpleasant. The woman gestured at a seat on a straight-backed chair and took her place in an armchair that screamed *I'm the one in control.*

I sat down gingerly on the edge of the seat, feeling too much like an errant schoolgirl for comfort. *Grow a pair, already, Mira. These people are the ones at fault, not you.*

"About The Creig—"

"I am The Creig of Clan Creig, the matriarch of the Highland Heathen Clan, kin to the first Vikings born of Fenrir, and Queen of the Northern Sea. And you are Miracle Camila Tala, the person who thinks to expose our clan to the world."

Huh. Well, that's not what I was unexpecting.

"I see ye dinna deny it," she said, drilling her fingernails on the arms of her chair.

"It was not my intention to offend you." What was I supposed to call her. Your Majesty? "Only to advance knowledge in the world."

Her eyes bore into mine. "And ye, a chit of a girl, think the world is ready for us." She shook her head in dismay. "Ye have no idea the problems meddling can cause. I demand ye cease this nonsense and destroy any evidence immediately."

"Excuse me. But who are you to tell me what to do?" Heat fired my bloodstream well past simmer to a roiling boil.

"I explained who I am. Why would ye do such a thing anyway? For fortune or fame? That's a pitiful reason to attack others."

I blushed hard at the accusation. She had me there. I did covet the fame. "It's not like that. You have me all wrong."

"Do I, Miss Tala? Then enlighten me. Why are ye doing this thing?"

I hedged my answer. "It's too late to stop now anyway. My friend Amy took credit for my work and put it on social media."

"Which calls your judgment *again* into question. I have no idea what my grandson sees in ye."

"Your grandson's Calan? Is he here?" To my dismay my heartrate doubled and my lower regions heated up at the mere mention of his name. God, I needed to get that under control. No way was I going to be attracted to a man who just threw me on an aircraft and tossed me to the wolves, by the look of this setup.

"He's expected momentarily. He had to clean up *yer* mess."

"My mess! I've had just about enough of your accusations, and if he's done anything to my friend, Amy, so help me God—"

"Grandmother, what's going on here? I could hear your voices all the way down the hallway."

A big guy stood in the doorway to the library. I did a double take—he looked so much like Calan...well, except for the traditional kilt that he wore with such flair. They sure grew them big in the Highlands.

"Grandson, stay out of this. It is my right to question this mortal looking to do our family harm."

"You must be Mira. Welcome to Castle Creigbourne," he said, ignoring his grandmother's edict and stepping forward to shake my hand. He looked so much like Calan that it brought everything back. The same incredible build, handsome face and long thick locks tied back. Only this guy wore a kilt with enough aplomb to raise a girl's skirts clear over her head. The intense personal connection with Calan between the sheets and the events of the past twenty-four hours that could only be called insane came rushing to the forefront. I pushed it all aside. I needed to keep my wits about me. What if this was another ruse and this man was just pretending to be nice?

The Creig's mouth firmed even more, if that were possible, while she glared at the two of us. "Lachlan Creig," she muttered with a shake of her head. "This errant child needs to be taken to task, not coddled."

"I'm certain we can come to some sort of compromise in due course."

"Sorry, but, other than being made to feel like a criminal, I do have some questions," I ventured. Finally, someone had arrived that *maybe* I could reason with.

"Do you mind if I borrow Mira for a few minutes, Grandmother?"

She nodded her regal head, bestowing her blessing. *Right.* She just wanted *my* head.

As soon as we were out of earshot, I spoke. "Thank you for rescuing me. That old lady is no lady! Now, I need to get out of here. I have a job waiting and I'm really late."

"*Never* call The Creig an old lady if you want to keep that pretty head on your shoulders!" He looked equal parts horrified and amused. "But I'm afraid you're not going anywhere until we have a wee talk."

My heart sank. Or *maybe* reasoning with the Creig clan was an impossibility?

Chapter Thirteen

Calan

Okay, with Mira safely on her way to Scotland, I could deal with loose ends in Vegas. Being separated from her at this vulnerable time in our relationship was not the best of things, but necessary. I'd hop a jet later and be with her soon, explain why I'd had to act so fast. Until then, my family would have her back, keep her safe from harm, if not from The Creig's sharp tongue. Mira was feisty though, making her a good match for my staunch grandmother, no doubt.

"You have arrived at your destination," the voice announced on the satnav system when I reached the front of a duplex. I continued driving around the block of the middle-class neighborhood, wanting to park out of sight, then slip back unseen to confront this Amy Stratton with how the real world worked when you betrayed a friend.

My cell rang just as I parked. *Cristaldo.*

"What the hell is going on? I thought you said this was contained. What the hell is the video doing all over the internet? And what are you doing about it?"

"The video is about to be proved a fake and will be down within the hour. You have my word on it."

"It better be! And what about this Mira Tala? Has that threat been eliminated?"

"It's in hand."

"I want a report back in one hour. Or the Tribunal will be getting involved."

"Threats are unnecessary. We're both wanting the same thing, Cristaldo. I'll call you as soon as I've dealt with the person responsible for the current situation."

"Fine."

We disconnected. *Okay. Time to focus on Miss Amy Stratton.* I knocked on the front door of the duplex, the side rented to Mira's former friend. She was inside, according to the GPS on her phone. It took a few extra loud knocks, but finally a pale face appeared in the window alongside the door.

Then, appearing to approve of my outward appearance, she opened the door.

"Yes. Can I help you?" she asked with a small smile. A woman of medium height, heavier build, she looked more like someone who worked at the zoo with animals than Mira did. No makeup, dark brown hair pulled into a tight ponytail and beige shorts with a shapeless white shirt.

"I'm looking to speak with Amy Stratton?"

"I'm Amy."

"I'm Calan Creig. May I come in? It's personal, about your friend Mira."

Her eyes widened in alarm. "Is she okay?"

"She's fine." *Better than fine.* Spectacular was a more appropriate word, but it was best I keep my mind on the matter at hand.

"Come in. Would you like something to drink? Coffee or something cold?" she asked, leading the way into the living room at the front of the house. She indicated the furniture and I sat on the sofa.

"No, I'm fine, thanks. This won't take but a few minutes."

She sat quite near me, which was a surprise since she didn't know me from Adam.

"So, you and Mira are friends?" she asked, interest lighting her expression.

"We are. Let me get right to the point."

She was fussing with her hair and pulled out the tie, allowing her locks to escape and fall to her sturdy shoulders. She fluffed them with her hands and grimaced. "I must look a sight. I haven't had time to put on any makeup today or anything."

"You look fine. Now, about your friend Mira."

"Where is she, by the way? I tried calling her phone and it went straight to voice mail."

"She's fine. Well, upset about the video, of course."

Amy had the grace to look abashed. "Yes, well, I'm sorry about that. I had a few drinks and it just kind of happened."

"I see. Well, you need to take it down. Say it was a hoax."

She frowned and stopped fiddling. "Why would I do that?"

"Because it's the right thing to do."

"Mira didn't ask me to do any such thing."

"That's because she's too upset. But if you want to keep your friend happy, I would suggest you fix this."

Amy began chewing on a cuticle. "I can't do that. I'd look like an idiot."

Worse than you do now? I couldn't imagine betraying a friend the way she had, but I couldn't say that aloud, so I gave it another shot. "Are you saying that your friend's feelings are unimportant to you? That having that video up means more to you than Mira?"

"No, of course not. Okay, I'll do it." She still looked undecided, which made me need to push this further.

"I need to see you do it."

"What? I can handle taking the video down myself." She looked at me suspiciously now.

But the clock was running out on this thing, and I needed to hurry it along. What worked better than money to encourage human cooperation? "I will pay you for your time, of course."

"Pay me. Why would you do that?" Her eyes widened.

"For goodwill. I'm rich. Trust me, I can afford it. And if you don't want to keep it, just donate it to the zoo. I'm certain they're always in need of charity. Do it in your own name and I'm fairly certain that will be seen in a good light by the community."

"Yes. Our campaigns to raise funds are ongoing. I would *love* to have my name engraved on the special plaque for Golden Trust donors in reception. How much are we talking about here?"

"What does a Golden Trust cost? Would a million cover it?'

"A million? *Holy shit,* what kind of background do you come from?" Amy looked far younger now, her eyes as rounded as a newborn owl's.

"Then I will have the money transferred as soon as I see the video discredited and taken down."

"Okay, it's your money. I'll be right back." She got up and retrieved her laptop. Sitting back on the sofa, she brought up the internet and her Facebook account. Her fingers flew over the keys as she made the necessary adjustments. "There. We happy?" She turned the computer around and indicated what she had done.

"Yes." I took out my phone and brought up my banking institution. "Now, just give me the particulars, and I'll be on my way."

She jumped up again and came back with some paperwork in hand. "I've sent them money before, just small sums. But this is going to knock their proverbial socks off." Her smug, self-satisfied smile spoke volumes.

I quickly completed the transaction. "Okay. All done. Thanks for your cooperation, Miss Stratton."

"Please, call me Amy. Now, how about a drink to celebrate?"

"I would enjoy that, but I'm running late for another meeting as it is. A CEO's job is never done," I said with a courteous smile to take the sting out of the rejection. All my instincts suggested that Amy Stratton would not take lightly to being pushed aside, that she had a bit of an inflated sense of self.

I wondered how the pair had met. Mira's moral compass was far stronger than her friend's. Well, opposites often hooked up. Were Mira and I opposites? I knew we shared chemistry that was off the charts. That I was already missing being with her. That she had totally turned my life upside down, making me rethink my priorities. But the one thing that stood out was that I'd take them all on before I'd let anyone harm a hair on her head.

"Yeah, I get that." Amy didn't bother to hide her disappointment. "Will you tell Mira to call me? I don't want to lose my bestie over a silly misunderstanding."

Misunderstanding? That was putting it mildly.

"I will do that." I got to my feet, more than ready to escape.

Amy jumped to hers and followed me to the door. She leaned against the door jamb, one hand twirling a strand of hair. It was then I caught her scent. Ugh. The woman was aroused.

"Thanks again." I said, stepping around her.

"Any time. You have my number."

Yes, I do. I took a breath of fresh air. The door stayed open behind me and when I reached the sidewalk in front of the duplex, I glanced back to see the woman still staring at me.

I nodded politely and strode off down the street, intent on getting back to Castle Creigbourne as soon as possible.

Chapter Fourteen

Mira

Calan's brother Lachlan gave me a serious look, making me wonder what his deal was. He had rescued me from The Creig, but the jury was still out on what his true intentions were.

"My question to you, Mira, is do you like to party?"

"What? *Party?*" I was confused by the question, and fairly certain my ears were deceiving me.

"Yes. You have just enough time to shower if you want because the fun is about to begin in the games room. All the family gets involved on games night." Lachlan's eyes lit up with pleasure at his announcement.

"I need to freshen up. But rather than games, could you just point the way to the nearest airport? I need to get home. I have a job."

"Well, here's the thing. We have to wait for Calan before you can fly home. He wants to speak with you first. Is that a problem for you? Our whole clan would enjoy spending time getting to know you for a few hours at least. And you are invited to stay as long as you wish, of course. Surely you have some vacation time you could use up?" There was a firmness behind his words that belied his easy speech.

"Just so we're clear on something else. Your clan—how do I say this without sounding all judgy... Okay, I'm a zoologist with a keen interest in cryptozoology, and Calan shared his status with me by showing me what he can do—you know—shift and change his molecular structure?"

"Right. Yes, we are all of the same bloodline, meaning we are all capable of the transformation."

"To wolves?" Even as I called it what it was, a shiver of dread raced down my spine.

Lachlan nodded. "There will be time for discussion later. My brother will fill you in on all you need to know, as is his right. He's just finishing a job in Vegas first."

"Okay then." I was nervous, sure. But suddenly the scope of this situation took root and I realized all that I could learn. How it could expand my knowledge base. This was *not* an opportunity to be missed. I just had to keep myself free from being influenced by Mr. McHottie. Like, no more intimate moments, AKA insanely-hot-mind-blowing sex.

I swallowed. Just the memory of that night together incinerated my panties. It still stung that he'd used me by not being clear from the beginning that he had an agenda. Yeah, we just met by coincidence at the storage lot. That event was as orchestrated as anything the CIA could pull off.

"Excellent. I hope you enjoy adult party games when you've got a few drinks under your belt? Because we've got a fun one planned for tonight that we hope you will join us in. It's meant to break the ice and welcome you to our home."

"Games?" Had I fallen into some kind of bizzarro universe next door? This clan was all werewolves, right? I rather expected we'd all go hunting on a full moon night, trying to bring down big game. I almost snorted, imagining The Creig as a she-wolf. Then, maybe it was not such a stretch—she had such a bad-ass attitude. "Sure, why not?"

Musing about how much I had to learn, I nearly missed Lachlan stopping our endless tramp through the castle and pointing out a closed door. "This is your suite. I'll send a servant to escort you back, say, in half an hour?"

"Works for me."

"Oh, and feel free to partake of any of the clothes or sundries."

"Thanks." I didn't have much in my carryall in the way of a nice outfit. Just a pair of jeans and a couple of T-shirts and fresh underwear.

Wondering what was behind the curtain, I entered the guest suite with high hopes. Disappointed? A definite no. Lovely huge windows were allowing in the last rays of sunlight to stream across the immaculate hardwood floor. The room was dominated by a gorgeous canopy bed featuring flowing ivory silk lace tied to the four engraved wooden posts. The thick-padded headboard just meant for relaxing against while reading a novel or two drew me like a magnet. I needed to shower, but first I had to just try out that bed that looked to be floating on air.

I climbed up onto the mattress fit for a princess, sinking into the scrumptious bedcovers. *Oh my, a gal could get used to this luxury in a New York minute.* Then I remembered my anger at being tossed on the plane without having a say in the matter and my anger returned with a vengeance. *Just wait until you get here, Mr. Calan Creig. You're going to get an earful.* I would be taking the next plane home.

Giving up the chance at research sucked, but I couldn't *ever* condone a man doing what he'd done. If I came back, and that was a big freakin' *if,* it would be on my own terms, and it would be my decision. *No man is in charge of me.* I'd made it this long in life without a father figure—I would walk the rest of this life on my own terms. Then I remembered how my *inheritance* was a box of damn drugs and I jumped off the bed. *Clean up and get on with things. Best thing for it.*

Twenty minutes later, with my hair up in a tidy updo and a dash of red gloss on my lips for courage, I exited the bathroom and stood in front of the armoire, trying to decide what to wear. *Wow. Some closet.* The Creig clan certainly had enough disposable income. All the items looked brand-new, and not cheaply made like my clothing that I always bought on sale or for a nominal sum at Goodwill.

Not that I was complaining. Fashion was well down on my list of needs. The zoo animals didn't care what I looked like, just that I was there to feed and care for them. Of course, that thought brought on another round of righteous anger for what Calan had done, interfering with my life. Then I remembered the men who had shown up at my door. Okay, it had been good at that moment to have some support, but I could have reasoned with them. *Found some money somehow. Maybe borrowed from a friend?* They wouldn't have offed me. They needed me alive to pay them back. It would have just been a warning.

Oh crap, look at the time! I pulled out a pair of skinny jeans that looked like they might fit and tugged them on, then paired them with a pretty white lace cold shoulder top that made me feel sexy. The castle must have central heating, because I was warm enough—I could have worn a bikini and gotten away with it. *Now that would cause a stir, playing an adult game in a bathing suit.* I snorted.

Probably not a good idea, considering the background of the clansmen. I mean, werewolves were notorious in literature for chasing women and claiming them. But who knew what the real deal was? It would be nice to separate fact from fiction. Maybe I could learn a little tonight before I headed home, so the trip and missing work were not a complete waste.

Pleased with my appearance for a change—I had even chosen a cute pair of shortie black suede boots that added height to my petite frame—I exited the suite. I had a good sense of direction, surely I could find my own way?

But I didn't need to. As soon as I opened the door, I was greeted by a young woman dressed in black pants and a white long-sleeved shirt that looked like a uniform. A courteous smile lit her face.

"I was about to knock, miss. Would you follow me to the games room, please?"

"Sure." I joined her. "I'm Mira, by the way."

"Sally. You look nice," she said, giving me a sideways glance as we strolled the hallway.

"Thanks. Have you worked here long?"

"Just over a year. I like it here. Everyone's polite. So often people with money seem to think they need to live up to the stereotype of being snotty and standoffish. Not the Creig clan. They treat their employees like family."

Was she also a werewolf? It wasn't something I could just blurt out. If she wasn't and got frightened at the idea, I would ruin it for her. She'd worked for a year already, and she was obviously fine. *Best to say nothing.*

"Here we are," Sally announced with a nod at the door marked *Games Room.*

"I guess I would have eventually found it," I said with a smile.

"True. I predict you'll have a good time this evening. The Creigs are known for their fun game nights."

"Thanks." I took a deep breath and opened the imposing door, prepared to face a roomful of strangers. At least for once, fashion had given me some confidence. What was that about clothes making a person? Maybe I had been lax in that direction, because walking in there, among a suspected group of werewolves, I held my head up high.

I was as good as them. It just hadn't come about from being born with a silver spoon in my mouth. *More like a cheap plastic spoon.* But I had made the best of it, not fallen into the quagmire of easy money from crime. I'd studied hard, earned a scholarship and paid my dues. And damn it, I was proud of that.

I took a quick look around at the group of strangers appearing to be having a good time, laughing and joking. Huge hot males seemed to dominate this clan. Four in total. I recognized Lachlan from earlier, grateful The Creig was absent. Maybe she was out having her ax sharpened? The cackling words, *double, double, toil and trouble* really captured her aura admirably. *Not nice, Mira.* She was an old lady who deserved respect just for making it to that age. *Yeah, maybe,* I countered. Wow, and there were some gorgeous females as well. I counted three women. Thank goodness I had dressed to fit in.

"Ah, Mira, good of you to join us." Lachlan came forward like I had all the choices in the world at my disposal and I had chosen to show up at their games night. His greeting drew everyone's attention my way, turning seven sets of eyes on me as I gave him a small, tight smile.

One of the females sashayed forward. "Hi, I'm Sherry, a long-time friend of Calan's." The way she said that with a special gleam in her eye gave me pause. Were they an item? Was he also hiding a girlfriend? My anger began to simmer again and I gave the woman a cooler look. Fortunately, another woman stepped up and gave me an easy grin.

"I swear this clan has more cousins than the backwoods of some southern county in North America. Hi, Mira. I'm Esme. Married to this hot hunk right here." She put her arm around Lachlan's waist and gave a quick squeeze. He leaned down to bestow a kiss. "Still on our honeymoon," she added with a smug smile as she came up for air.

"Get a room guys," one of the males hooted with a whistle. I couldn't help but smile at the guy. I soon learned he was Logan, another brother. So Calan had two brothers, Lachlan and Logan, and endless cousins, the two in attendance tonight being named Toby and Connor. The final female was Isla, another cousin.

"Nice to meet you all." I prayed I could keep all the names straight.

"Okay," Lachlan said, rubbing his hands together. "Someone grab the Macallan and let's join round."

We all did as he bid, actually getting comfortable sitting in a small circle on the thick plush rug in front of the well-stocked bar area.

"This game is called Never Have I Ever. Have you played it before, Mira? Do I need to explain the rules?"

I shook my head. I'd had no time for games in university, always working part-time to pay for things my scholarship didn't cover, and had always felt I missed out on the true college experience. "Please do."

"The first player starts the game by saying 'Never have I ever...' to be followed by something he or she has never done before. Or recites what's on the card. Then everyone who *has done* whatever he or she said must drink. Clear?"

I nodded, intrigued by the idea. At least it would take my mind off my predicament and maybe buy me some goodwill with this group. "Sure, sounds like fun."

Shot glasses were set in front of all of us while Lachlan began shuffling some printed cards.

"Okay, we'll start with Sherry and go around the room clockwise."

Sherry picked up the top card and read it out loud, a coy smile curving her lips. "Never have I ever lied in my life."

That was easy. Everyone held out their shot glasses to be filled with the golden whiskey, its fine fragrance filling the air with the scent of honey and chocolate with a hint of spice. My mouth watered. But duh, who hasn't lied at least once in their lives? White ones keep society running smoothly. The whiskey was excellent going down, warming my stomach. I hoped there would be snacks soon as it also wetted my appetite.

I glanced at Logan, who was looking at me. He smiled, lighting up his green eyes. They reminded me so much of Calan's. I looked around, realizing everyone had those magnetic eyes. *Right. All related, all probably shifters. Crap.* What if one of them took it into their mind to bite me? Would I become a werewolf at the next full moon? I shook my head to dispel the compelling image.

"Never have I ever kissed someone younger than me," Logan announced, his turn to pick a card.

I groaned. No drink this time. Then I remembered Johnny Porter from junior high school. Right, he'd been one month younger than me and we'd kissed behind the gym bleachers.

I held out my glass again, enjoying my second drink as much as the first. But maybe I'd better slow down? I hadn't had much to eat today, a bit busy getting abducted and thrown on a plane. The liquor tempered my anger though, keeping my nerves soothed.

"Oh, this one is good!" Esme said, giving her hubby a light punch on the upper arm. Boy oh boy, but all the guys in this group had good muscle development. "Never would I ever kiss Chris Hemsworth or Ryan Gosling."

"I would kiss both of them in a heartbeat," Toby said. "More if they'd ask. I mean, I like women, but those men—I got a serious bro-romance going on there!"

Everyone laughed and the women had another shot, along with Toby.

It was my turn and I took a card eagerly. The room had developed nice soft edges and my mind had relaxed for the first time in ages. Now I understood my colleagues at university. They just had to put some things out of their minds for a bit.

"Your turn, Mira," Lachlan said, pointing at the cards.

"Never have I ever believed in The One, a fated or Forever Mate."

Huh. Did I believe there was one perfect person in the world for me? Calan's image came to mind and I shook it away with prejudice. It would take more than one amazing tumble in bed to come to that conclusion. But I was far more curious about this group. Did they believe that?

Everyone around me held out their shot glasses and they all turned to look at me with keen interest. What was this? Some kind of test? Okay, call me a sucker, but I did believe in true love, that there was only one man for me that I might or might not find in this lifetime. I mean, what were the chances, really?

Oh, what the hell. I didn't want to be excluded though I'd had more than enough alcohol and would be regretting this in the morning. It wasn't often I'd allowed myself to indulge this much, but it was nice to blur the edges of my reality, even if for a short time.

I held out my glass to approving looks from everyone except Sherry. What was her problem?

Sally, the young woman I'd met earlier appeared in the room and began laying out trays of fresh sandwiches and bowl of snacks around our circle, drawing everyone's attention. Great, I needed to absorb some of this alcohol. I grabbed a nice thick ham and Swiss cheese and began stuffing it in my mouth. I moaned at the amazing taste of the fresh baked rye bread. No one noticed, too busy eating with abandon.

I liked this family, more than I had expected. My stomach took a tumble as I thought of my own brother still on the lam, wishing he were home safe and sound. If only I had the funds to have someone search for him, but I was skinned just trying to pay his debts, so in reality there was nothing I could do for him right now. Then I remembered that Evan's debt had been paid, by the very man I was ready to burn in effigy, taking some of the heat out of my anger.

My hunger sated, I watched with amusement as the other people in the room joked and laughed as they continued consuming a gazillion calories without one guilty look on anyone's face. Maybe staying a few days in Scotland wouldn't be so bad. As long as Calan stayed out of the picture. The bone I had to pick with him was going to cause an uproar.

Chapter Fifteen

Calan

Pissed at how long it was taking to get home on the jet, I drummed my fingers on the armrest. I fought the urge to scream at the pilot to get us there already, but I resisted, knowing he had to be conscious of safety first. I needed to see Mira in the worst way. To explain. If I'd had any doubt she was my one, it had been dispelled having her so far away. The drive to get back to her took over my mind, the urgent need to touch her, make love to her making me antsy like never before, though the question remained—what was I going to do about not wanting a committed relationship?

But even more pressing was the need to straighten out the situation with Mira, to protect her from the wrath of fellow weres. If she couldn't be made to see reason, what the hell was I going to do about it? I loved my job as enforcer and head of security for our clan. But not stopping Mira exposing werewolves to the larger world could be seen as a dereliction of my sworn oath to protect the clan and all werewolves against known threats.

But causing her difficulties in her chosen occupation also rubbed me the wrong way. She had a right to choose her path, just I had to keep that from interfering with my objectives. Quicksand awaited the unwary. How to keep one of us from being the target for the Tribunal?

A growing realization that I might have to make a choice loomed. *Her career or mine.* But first I had to try reasoning with her. Come clean and explain that to be together, we needed to come to a compromise. Because damn it, I could not imagine a future now without her in it. The need to see her, growing stronger by the minute, proved the case.

The sound of the engines changing their high-pitched whine alerted me to the fact we were about to land. *Thank Christ.* Now I could get on with things.

I leapt from the plane, not bothering with the stairs, and raced across the landscape toward the castle. The full moon rising over the battlements caused the ancient pull to wolf and an insistent pressure to shift. *Yes, I promise.* I would transform later, join my brothers and cousins for a midnight run. But first, I had to see Mira.

I followed her smoking-hot scent and burst into the games night room. What was going on? Everybody looked half corked, laughing and having a merry old time. Mira sat amongst my brothers, sister-in-law and cousins, a smile lighting her gorgeous face as she looked at Logan. Then she turned and spotted me, her expression instantly changing. Her beautiful blue eyes filled with a hot anger like she wanted to thrust a dagger into my still-beating heart. I stopped dead in my tracks, my breathing rapid from rushing to her side.

Why was she so damned angry? I had only sent her here to keep her safe. And why had she been smiling at my brother? Jealousy rose, hot and bitter in my mouth. I needed a damn drink. I strode over to the bar and filled a glass with whiskey, taking a huge gulp to calm my nerves.

"Calan, good to see you, bro." Lachlan appeared at my side. He poured himself a shot of the liquor and turned to survey me. "How you doing? How was the flight?"

"Fine," I said through gritted teeth.

"Okay. We've been working on getting to know Mira. Did you know she believes in fated mates?"

"I take it you were playing that drinking game?"

"What better way to get to know someone than over a bottle of Scotland's finest? Everything okay? You seem a little off."

"I'm fine."

"Great. Good thing you're not a female. *Fine* generally means trouble's brewing when it's been said, and you've just repeated it. Something you're not sharing? Want to go to my office and talk about it?"

"No, I do not want to talk. I would prefer to have another drink then go for a run. You up for it?"

"Sure." Lachlan leaned in closer, though the laughter from the others would have easily covered up our conversation. I kept my eyes on my glass, ignoring the antics. "We like your lass. She's spirited."

"You don't know the half of it." I drained the liquor and poured another shot.

"Maybe you'd better spend some time with Mira before we head out. She's watching you with rather a lot of anger in her eyes. I take it she didn't voluntarily come here?"

"No. But she was in danger." I shrugged. "What choice did I have? She wouldn't listen to reason."

"Aww, well it's a difficult time in any Forever Mate relationship. And yours, well, let's say has more problems than most to figure out. She's human, she's working against our cause, she's spirited and too beautiful for her own good. That about cover it?"

"You forgot loyal to a fault, good at her job and wanting fame in her occupation." Damn, but this relationship was going to cost one of us something of vital importance.

"Maybe you can use that loyalty to explain things? Surely, she'd understand duty to family—ours included?" Lachlan asked, his expression thoughtful.

"I'm thinking I might have to be the one here who's willing to give up the most in this situation. But why are we talking about this?" Though I was beginning to see there might be only one real answer to our dilemma, I didn't want to say it out loud or even think it yet. Maybe I could have a few days of peace before acting on it?

"I'm here when you want to discuss it."

I nodded. "Thanks. Now I should find grandmother."

"Before she finds you and chews you a new one," Lachlan said with a grin.

"Precisely. And don't forget our run. I'll make it quick."

I skirted the group of players and headed for the door. Striding down the hall, I was surprised to hear footfalls behind me.

"Calan. Stop! We need to talk." Mira's voice rang out.

I turned and crossed my arms over my chest, unable to meet her eyes. I still hadn't forgotten her look when she'd spotted me earlier. It hurt, maybe even more considering what I was willing to do for her.

"Yes?" I said, with all the nonchalance I could manage considering all I wanted to do was to sweep her into my arms. Why in the hell did my Forever Mate have to be a woman who refused to see reason?

"I can see you're angry. But damn it, I was thrown on a plane and—"

"For your own good. You were in mortal danger," I interrupted. "So frightened that you passed out from all the stress. What was I to do? I knew my family would be able to look to your needs while I sorted out the situation in Vegas."

"Yeah, about that. I don't think The Creig likes me one bit. But, still, I should still have been given a choice. To wake up alone on the plane—" She looked incensed at the memory.

"Did Alistair not go with you?" Now I was confused.

"Well, yeah, so to wake up on a plane with a stranger—"

"Alistair's a good man." Did she think I would send her off with a monster? Is that what she thought of me? Unease crept into my mind. Had she not felt what I had when we made love? Not experience the bonding of two mortal souls? Maybe I was the one who wasn't remembering it correctly?

"I know that now." She rubbed her forehead like it hurt and swayed a bit.

I rushed to her side to support her. "Are you okay?"

"Too much to drink."

"Let's get you to bed."

"But weren't you off to do something?"

"It can wait a few minutes." I put my arm around her slender shoulders and began to lead her to the room I had asked be prepared for her. *Torture, being so close to Mira.* Her scent alone triggered something deep within me. But she had been drinking and I could not, would not, take advantage of the situation.

"I can find my own way, damn it!" She shrugged my arm off and weaved down the hallway, keeping me on edge.

"Didn't they feed you?" I asked, concerned.

"Duh. By the way, your family is so nice. Well, except for that old lady..."

"I'd be careful about calling my grandmother an old lady."

"It would probably be best then if our paths don't cross. She was ready to bite my head off earlier. In fact, I suspect she's out back sharpening her ax. Remember Lizzy Borden? And my skinny neck's not going to take forty wacks."

"No one here would ever harm you. You have my word on that." I stiffened at the slanderous idea. Who did she think we were? Uncivilized we are not. I pushed down the anger at her comments and focused on getting Mira to her room.

"Sorry, I don't actually think that. I'm sure she's a sweetheart under the right conditions. I'm just a little put off because some idiot threw me on a plane and plunked me down in the land of wolves." Her voice grew louder. "And none of this makes any damn sense!" She stumbled and that was too much. I swept her up into my arms, breathing in the amazing scent that was Mira and bore her down the hallway.

"Put me down!"

I ignored her ridiculous objections and continued onward, then kicked open her bedroom door before laying her on the bed.

She glared at me, her lips pursed with anger. The memory of kissing and tasting those lips stirred something primal in me and it was all I could do not to fall on her and take her right then and there. I raked a hand through my hair. Last thing I wanted to do was to make this situation worse. I needed to calm my mate down, not do anything to rile her more, though making love was the very thing we needed. She was aroused by me, whether she would admit it or not. *Probably not at the moment.*

I found the strength to take off her shoes and pull the covers up over her, tucking her in.

"Sleep. We'll talk in the morning when you're calmer."

"I won't be any calmer. I'll just have longer to stew. How could you do that? Just toss me on a plane when you know how much my job means to me."

Her eyes riveted me, filled with not only anger but a hint of hurt at her thinking I had betrayed her. To my mind I had not. I wanted nothing but the best for her. It was a decision made in the moment, one that took her out of the equation to keep her safe.

"I did what I thought best. Tomorrow we can talk. Work this out."

"You can talk until you're blue in the face for all I care, but I'm still going home. I'll not give up on my dreams just because you say so."

"I'm not asking you to give up on your dreams. But damn it, what if your dreams cause a firestorm that could consume all of us? Is that what you want? To destroy all the Creig clan has built over the centuries? Would that make you happy? You become famous, but the rest of us pay the price?" I should have stopped myself long before this, but it spilled out. Frustration had grown to epic proportions.

I had to get out of here before I said something or did something that could destroy all hope of us getting our relationship back on track. I hurried to the door, hearing her weak protests before striding away. I needed to run. Now. Then I remembered I also need to speak with The Creig. I gritted my teeth and headed for her wing of the castle.

"Grandson." My grandmother leveled her gaze my way as I entered her chamber. I kissed her cheek and took a seat nearby. She was busy sitting at her desk writing a letter. A common event for The Creig. She didn't trust the internet or social media. She had a point. Look at the fiasco it had landed us in.

"I trust you are feeling well, Grandmother?"

"No thanks to that Mira person. What were ye thinking bringing her here?" She wrote a few more lines in her perfect calligraphy handwriting with the nib point pen she swore by.

I took a deep breath. "She means a lot to me."

That made her stop writing entirely, set down the pen and turn her full attention my way. She sighed after looking into my eyes and taking in my truth. "It's that way, is it? Well, this needs sorting. I trust ye have a plan, Grandson?"

I nodded, though I was uncertain of how best to proceed. I needed time with Mira first. "I need a few days to flesh things out, but I'm quite certain the threat will be nullified in short order."

"It better be. Yer freedom is at risk. And what this could do to our clan—" She shook her head with dismay. "Now go and have that run you need. You look about ready to burst into flames."

"Aye." I got to my feet, thankful I'd gotten off lightly.

On the way out of the castle, I shed my clothing, arriving naked under the rising moon. Taking a deep breath of heather and moss that stirred good memories of many times running together with my brothers under a canopy of ancient stars, I began to lope across the landscape, keeping an eye out to avoid an ambush. I needed to feel a part of things tonight, focus on wearing off the excess energy that wanting to bed Mira had caused.

I had just entered the edge of the forest when a scent drifted in on the night breeze of a wolf I would prefer not to encounter. My cousin Sherry. Though surely by now she would have caught on that I was taken, that my Forever Mate had arrived at Castle Creigbourne. Even if Mira and I were at odds at the moment, it would surely not stay that way. There had to be a way out of this mess. A plan of action that would accomplish all my goals in one fell swoop.

I shook my head. Enough with the thinking. I needed to run, feel the wind, be the wolf. Capture the essence. *Alive, strong and free.*

Lower to the ground now as predator, the scents of nocturnal creatures tempted me to the chase, and I bounded across the landscape, my giant paws eating up the distance. I wanted this for Mira. To know how incredible it was to be wolf. I quickly broke my own rule about stopping ideas from taking over my brain and instead focused on the riveting quandary.

Was it a possibility? I knew of the amazing find of the Lupus Sanguis Chalice by the Luceres scholars, Alessandro and Maximus. They'd tracked it down in the Arctic, the legendary chalice that could save a human bitten by a werewolf during the first full moon. It had saved their Forever Mate Trinity's life when she was bitten by a Nomad.

My heart beat quicker, imagining sharing this magnificence with Mira. Surely such a gift would sway her to our side? I was so involved with the idea, I almost smacked into Sherry, the last wolf I wished to meet up with.

She gave me a playful push with her paws, keeping her claws well in check. A signal to play. No one else was around yet, making me wonder where my brothers had gotten to? We'd had plans to meet up. Not wanting to be seen as unfriendly to another member of our clan, I stopped myself from brushing her off and instead focused on running along ahead of her. Soon enough she'd tire of the pace and head back. My endurance was legendary and necessary. An enforcer needed to stay in top form, protect his clan, and keep the faith.

Chapter Sixteen

Mira

Sunlight streaming in the window woke me mid-morning, groggy with a pounding headache. My mind went back to the night before, remembering the drinking game then Calan hauling my ass to bed. I was all alone now in a tangle of sheets, mouth parched and body in need of a shower. I forced myself to a sitting position and spotted a bottle of water at my beside.

Twisting the cap off, I gulped it down, easing the pain. *Right. Get cleaned up, then demand to be taken home.*

I headed into the bathroom and turned on the water, pleased to find everything a gal needed at hand. In short order I was halfway presentable and ready for some fresh air, dressed in an outfit that made me feel rather pretty, a midi-length red wool dress that draped beautifully over my curves. I'd even found a pair of stylish black dress boots in soft suede to complement the look.

"Okay. Now we can face them," I announced to the mirror, adding a dash of lipstick and mascara.

Leaving the room, I strolled down the hall, intent on checking out all Creigbourne had to offer. Why not? I'd never get a chance to see over an actual castle again in my lifetime. I'd bet on that. It hadn't been at all what I'd expected so far. Calan was so modern in his dress, though his brothers were not— Logan, Lachlan and the cousins had worn kilts last night.

But the castle made me feel like I'd stepped back a thousand years. I admired the suits of chain mail, claymore swords, battleaxes, bows and arrows and other weapons of the warrior that lined the stone walls. Did they still use some of these today? Some looked recently honed, and I shivered at how sharp some of the devices appeared. I could only imagine the power of holding a double-sided ax over the head of those threatening my brother. *Too bad that's frowned on in modern times.* The image of Calan's stoic grandmother came to mind. Maybe we had more in common than I'd first considered. Afterall, she was defending her own family. I should give the woman another chance—with Calan now in residence, it was unlikely she'd do me in, right?

"I trust you rested well?" Calan asked, strolling up to me as I ran my fingers over the edge of one of the broadswords to very, very carefully check its edge. *Yup, scary as Hades.*

"No thanks to you." I wasn't letting him off the hook any time soon. Even if he did look as sexy as hell in a kilt, and the first time I'd seen him in one. It more than suited him, making me want to run my hands up his well-shaped legs to discover the truth of what a Scotsman wore under it. *No, get a grip.* He needed to know I meant business. "Do you use these anymore?" I pointed at the display of swords.

"Yes, on occasion."

I turned to catch him grimacing. "What is it? You don't like to be called out?" I narrowed my eyes at him, imagining winding a rope around him and tying him up in knots, so he got the idea of what it felt like to be toyed with. I might leave him a knife to cut himself free. *Or not.*

"I needed you to see reason. You were so hellbent on becoming famous that you didn't give a thought to those you would harm in the process."

That hurt. "I would never harm anyone intentionally. How could you think that? I realize we hardly know anything about each other, but I would never do that. Not for fame. Or for fortune. So, explain to me what the big deal is here."

He gave me an unfathomable look, like he was truly weighing his words. "How about I show you instead? Could we just put down our swords for a couple of days while I introduce you to my life? Let me show you what matters to me? To my clan?"

I pursed my lips. "Okay. But I'm not committing to changing my mind anytime soon. We clear? And I need to contact work, let them know I won't be in."

"That can be arranged. I just ask you keep an open mind."

"That's what scientific minds do, Mr. Creig."

"You telling me that all the educated minds you've met have been open to new ideas? Tell that to Alfred Wegener and his rejected theory of Continental Drift that was later proved true. Or Ignaz Semmelweis, who insisted hand washing would save lives. Do you realize how many women died in the past during childbirth due to lack of hygiene? Or genetic inheritance proposed by Gregor Mendel—"

"Enough! You've blowing my mind with all these facts, especially after a night playing the drinking game. And I think you forgot Nicholas Copernicus. You're not the only brainiac in the room, you know. I have studied a lot. I think the best minds are not just tunneled in on only one speciality but have some broad understanding of how the world works too."

"So, we do agree on something. Good start, *thasgaidh.*"

I ignored what sounded like an endearment. I'd look it up later. "Okay. But could I have some breakfast first? I'm about starved."

"Of course. Big breakfasts are a clan speciality. One not to be missed."

Calan remained silent as we walked down the hallway and I eyed him. Damn, but he looked good this morning. Even with the loogy feeling left from overindulging last night, I could see why Sherry fancied him. *Too damn handsome and confident for his own good.* What was he hiding behind that shiny veneer? Most women would be too blown away by him showing any interest in them to take him to task. Bet he'd never had a woman want to berate him like I had been doing.

Was that the attraction? The fact I was not available? But to be honest, I felt that attraction too. My whole body seemed to want to rub up against him though it was not going to happen. *Answers.* Those were my priority. Not spending time messing up the bedsheets, awesome as that sounded. *Nope. Not going to happen.*

But then he took my hand with a disarming smile, and my breath skittered as the warmth of him raced up my arm and sparked through my entire body. Damn, but this wasn't going to be a walk in the park. More like a ginger tiptoe through a bloody minefield. I couldn't wait to see what blew up next. Since we'd met nothing had stayed the same. Would I ever get my life back as it was in Vegas before this huge distraction came along? Sure, he'd saved my ass a couple of times. But he always went too far. Like what the hell was I doing in Scotland?

I had to stay on high alert. Not let Calan know how very much I was attracted to him. Otherwise, I had a sinking feeling I was going to lose something very dear to me and not have anything to replace it with. Like making my own mark in the world as I'd always dreamed of. *Focus on that, Mira, not on how good you feel touching him. Or when he touches you.*

We turned a corner and entered what I presumed was the dinning room.

"Good morning, you two. Glad you could join us," Logan said with a hearty welcome. Everyone from the night before was seated at a humongous wooden table that looked like it had been in the same spot for a thousand years just like the castle. Well, who could move such a beast? It seemed to be made of one giant piece of solid wood with huge carved legs that ended in lion's paws that sank into the gray slate floor.

I responded to all the greetings and sat where indicated. Wow, but the table was loaded with enough food to feed a barracks filled with soldiers. Werewolf lore suggested they had huge appetites, but nowhere had it been suggested they ate like this. The tantalizing scents drifting off the piles of steaks, sausages and ham slices, the cinnamon rolls and bowls of scrambled eggs, plates of fluffy omelets, flaky pastries, and even platters of fresh fruit and assorted cheeses made my mouth water insanely.

I love to cook, provide well for my guests, but I'd never seen such a sight as this outside a wedding reception. *Such a luxury.* It must be nice to have this all the time, I thought, looking around at all the happy, animated faces. No one seemed affected by a hangover. Mine fortunately was fading and I filled my plate with no hesitation. It wasn't often someone else cooked a meal for me. Probably never, if I was being honest.

I had been focusing so hard on the visuals that I missed something. Calan nudged me with a twinkle in his eyes. He had been watching me attack a particularly tender omelet filled with colorful peppers and sweet onions and fresh mozzarella cheese with the enthusiasm of one of our hungry zoo animals.

"What? I have something on my face?" I grabbed for the napkin sitting on my lap, rubbing at my lips.

"No. Esme was just inquiring if you like country fairs?"

I looked at her, sitting across the table beside her husband, and blushed at my inattention. In my defense, I was hungry. Hungry for more than food, but sustenance would have to do. *No jumping anyone's bones while you're in Scotland. We clear, Mira?* "Yes, of course. They're fun."

"Great. It's a family tradition attending the Spirit of Creigbourne festival each year. Should be interesting to revisit the soothsayer's booth? Remember what it led to the last time, Lachlan?" she said, teasing her husband with a come-hither glance I envied.

I mean, the pair was so in love it filled the room with a contentedness I'd never and would probably never experience in my lifetime.

"Aye. Marrying the most charming lass in Scotland."

"What, not the most charming lass in the world?" she asked, lightly swatting her husband's forearm.

"That goes without saying," he said.

"If I remember correctly, the old crone did say something about red-gold hair and a horse, Calan?" Logan said, his mouth turned up in a smirk, his eyes expressing his glee. "Black stallion, wasn't it? Do you ride, Mira?"

"Me?" I asked around a mouthful of food so delicious I was eating above my fighting weight. "Yes, of course. Many zoologists do, as point of fact. I don't own one though I hope to one day. I've rented a property that is big enough, though I'd want a pair as one can get lonely. My director at the Las Vegas Zoo has an amazing black Friesian walking horse. Very flashy with that unique four-beat running walk. Black Beauty, he calls him. Not original, but fitting."

"Well, fancy that," Logan said, looking pointedly at Calan.

Sherry frowned. She had been quiet during breakfast and had been only watching things. Maybe she wasn't all that pleased I was there, since I suspected she liked Calan more than she was letting on, though her next words suggested she'd thrown down the gauntlet. "I ride horses and have red-gold hair if anyone has noticed?"

"Ah, but do you come from the land of desert and sage, lovely Sherry?" Logan asked, his eyes suggesting he was not used to letting stuff go.

The discomfort was growing in the room, and I thought to dispel it. So far it had been fun and I didn't want to see things changed on my account. After all, none of them were to blame for my predicament, just the man who sat so stoically at my side.

"What do you do, Sherry? By the way, I love your hair. You do a much nicer style than I can manage." I lifted up my braid for emphasis. Hers was beautifully curled in waves and flowed down her back like a heroine in a romance novel. Something I'd never achieved in my wildest dreams.

"I own a series of boutiques specializing in giving a woman the full spa experience."

"That's great! Impressive, too."

She cocked her head sideways, as if assessing if it were possible to fix me somehow. "I think we could help you out. A full-day makeover. How does that sound?"

Less exciting than the fair, in truth. I'm not a damn science project. Then I realized that was rather how I saw this group, and mortification suddenly made me uncomfortable. Just because they might be werewolves didn't mean they weren't human beings first. Exposing their secret was not beneficial to them. Only to me. I squirmed in my seat, my hunger vanishing.

"Don't change a thing." Calan spoke up, grabbing my hand and squeezing it. "You're perfect as you are, Miracle Tala."

His touch stirred me, grounding me while at the same time sending a yearning through my veins of wanting more. *So much more.* The sensation made the outer edges of the room vanish until it was just him and I inside the circle, his penetrating glance seeming to go right through me, binding us. My brain went to mush, incapable of holding another thought. Riveted, my glance lingered, locked with his as his thumb gently circled my palm, sending delicious thrills of desire to my core. If the touch of his hand could bring on so much, what would it be like to be lying together again…

Conversation must be continuing around us. I had to pay attention or they'd think I'd gone daft. I made to tug my hand away and was grateful, but honestly, a bit bereft when Calan let me. But his eyes promised more. I shook my head. I had to stay in control of this, not be swayed by my libido. That wasn't the solution, right?

"Why is it women think soon as they've caught a man's eye it's time to fix something that doesn't need fixing?" Logan grumbled.

"If you think men are in control of how we look, think again," Sherry said, with a raised eyebrow.

I squirmed in my seat, wanting nothing more than to head out, then jumped up. "I need some fresh air. I think last night's overindulgence is still lingering," I said by way of explanation.

"I'll go with you." Calan stood too.

"No need. I'll just be a little while."

Of course he didn't take no for an answer, but instead took my hand again and led me away from the table, tucking my hand under his arm. *Not helping*.

"Don't forget we have the fair in half an hour," Esme called after us.

Calan waved her off and we headed outside together. The weather was fair enough, not nearly as warm as Vegas but the sun was trying to break through the clouds over the castle.

"Are you warm enough?" he asked.

I was shivering, though not from the cold.

"I'm fine," I said through gritted teeth. I caught him grinning down at me.

"What?"

"I feel it too, Mira. I want you so badly my teeth ache from it. But we need this time. We started so quickly, like two stars colliding, and now we have to find our way. It's not just us at stake here, it's our whole way of life."

"You keep saying you'll explain your side of things. So, explain. I already can see that you have an amazing life, an incredible family." I stopped walking and confronted him.

"Do you really believe that if you expose that we're not like other people, that we have secrets that could threaten the rest of the world, that everyone will just let us be?"

"I don't see it that way. The world deserves to know you exist. That all those myths and legends are true in some way. Maybe studying what makes you who you are can help others?"

"Hogwash. Studying us is not going to help anybody, least of all humans. We live in harmony because we keep our secrets and don't threaten anyone." He raked a hand through his hair. "We're stronger, smarter, quicker. Humans will resent that. Want to take, take, take what is not theirs. You have to realize that. We just want to live in peace as we've done for a thousand years. Not be held up as some kind of science project. Look at mankind's history, if you can stand to. Don't you all have a record of destroying what you don't understand?"

"Then let us understand," I pressed. "Help me to do this right. We can control this." I had to persuade him though I had to admit he had some valid objections.

"No." He shook his head vehemently, his mouth thinning. "I will not let our lives here be threatened in any way by anyone, not even you for you, Mira, as much as you already mean to me."

"What are you talking about? I'm a free agent. If I want to leave, I'll leave. It's against the law to try to stop me," I said, narrowing my eyes at Calan. I scanned the area, wondering which way I should run. It wouldn't come to that, would it? He'd treated me so well, helping with all my problems in Vegas, but he had sent me here without consulting me.

"All you care about is being famous. You don't care who you hurt in the process."

"That's not true! No one's going to hurt you." His words held some merit, and I knew I needed to do some soul searching. Perhaps I was too quick to want to capitalize on my accidental discoveries back in Vegas? Confused, I stood frozen to the spot.

"I'm more worried about you," he said, his tone softer.

"What do you mean?"

"I didn't want to have it come to this. But your stubbornness is leaving me no choice."

"Explain. I'm sick of not knowing everything about this situation. You keep hinting at things and it's driving me mad."

"Fine. Let's sit down for this." He strode away and I trailed along behind him.

Calan patted the spot beside him on one of the stone benches that graced the property, and I sat, as far away as the space allowed.

"Okay. It's a long story but for brevity's sake—we don't have long before someone will come to find us to open the festival—I'll give you the short form for now. But all werewolves are answerable to a governing body located in your hometown of Vegas. The Tribunal. It judges all of us, lays out punishments as it sees fit to offending members, works to keep our existence secret."

"Like a government?" Intrigued, I leaned in.

"Exactly like a government, only for paranormals. It's an ancient order that's done its job expertly over the centuries. It's only been the last couple hundred of years that it's been based in the United States. What it says, goes. It's the law."

"Are you saying they know about me?" I startled, worry overtaking my interest in a split second.

He nodded. "That's why I brought you here. To keep you safe."

"From the Tribunal? You mean they would harm me?" Aware my voice was turning high-pitched, I took a deep breath.

"I am the one in charge of finding out about you, to assist you in seeing reason to let this go. I'm my clan's enforcer and one of a select team of experts that compose the Worldwide Security for Lycans or WSL. I'm expected to clean up things like that, to keep my fellow shifters safe at all costs."

"You mean that you have to talk me out of exposing you? But what if you can't do that? What happens next?" Horrified by his words, my hand fluttered to my throat. To think that I had been the target from day one. That Calan had only come to see me to stop me from doing anything to expose his clan. Had everything been an act? His way of controlling me? But he could have just turned me in. Instead, he'd brought me to relative safety. Now I was more confused about how I saw it all. I needed time. Time to think this thing through properly.

"But I would never let the Tribunal do anything to you. You've become important to me, Mira. I'm falling for you and I want us to be able to move forward. Put all this behind us. Come to a compromise that will protect everyone, but especially you."

His words gave me hope that it was more than his just needing to do what his job entailed when it came to me. Although that didn't mean I wasn't upset. *Damn right I am.* It was all so much to take in. I wanted to step away from it, look at it with fresh perspective. But with Calan sitting so close, it only added confusion to the whole thing. What was the right thing to do in a situation like this? I'd bet I was the only human on planet Earth that had ever faced this insane dilemma. It was exhilarating and frightening at the same time.

I glimpsed a flash of movement to our right.

"Aw, there you two are. The festival is beginning and we need your attendance. Lachlan is about to give his speech," Logan said, coming up, glancing from me to his brother. "Everything okay?"

"Fine," we both said in unison and stood. The jury was still out on what was going to happen, but at least I now knew where I stood in the scheme of things…and it was not a place I ever wanted to be. *The razor's edge.* Like if I made the wrong move now, the situation would become damaged beyond salvation.

I shivered even as Calan again took my hand, squeezing it as if to give me comfort, his eyes shining with some kind of belief. Maybe it would be okay with such a man, a true alpha, wanting what was best for me? If that were indeed true? Again, I was overwhelmed with so much change, with no time to assimilate it. Perhaps he was right on one thing though—we needed to set things aside for a day or two, get to know each other more, and see a path forward that worked for everyone.

What else was there for it?

"You're in for a treat today, Mira," Logan said as the three of us trooped across the green space together.

"How so?"

"The famous Soothsayer of Lochness has set up a booth again this year. Esme and Sherry managed to snag an appointment for you to have a session with her. The old woman is Sherry's great-grandmother, so it was easy to arrange."

"Great. That sounds like fun," I said. At least it would take my mind off the present.

Calan gave his brother a look I couldn't interpret. I rather envied the history that was obvious between the siblings, so solidly here for each other. My mind couldn't help but compare it with Evan's and mine. Where was he right now? Was he okay? Fresh worries flooded my mind and I took a misstep.

"You okay?" Calan asked, instantly more attentive.

"I'm fine." Distracted, I blinked away the image of Evan on the last day we'd been together. The wistful look in his eyes as he tried to reassure me he was doing better. I needed to get him into rehab and the award money I would receive from my discovery would be the ticket to get that help.

"You can tell me anything, Mira. You know that right?"

"Can I?" I asked softly, looking at the far distance on the ocean now visible from our new location. The horizon seemed to have vanished into a soft haze, indistinct sky and water, a nonplace where secrets hide.

Perplexed, he took both my hands in his and nodded at his brother to go ahead.

"What is it? What's worrying you? Is it work? Your brother? Please, tell me. I can't help you if I don't know what's wrong."

Tears welled in my eyes. Not many people I had just met would care enough to ask. My anger at the situation drained away. "Work can do without me for a few days."

"So, it's Evan? Did you learn something about him recently?"

"No. That's the problem. I've been watching you and your brothers and cousins, and you're all so close and I don't know how Evan's doing. If he's okay or not?" I forced the words past the lump in my throat.

"I don't want you worrying about that. We can fix this. I'll have someone look into it today."

I shook my head, though a part of me appreciated the support. "I don't have the money for a private detective or I would have engaged one already."

"I wouldn't think of asking you for a cent to pay toward my providing *anything* you need."

I stiffened. "I always pay my own way."

"I mean no harm. I just want what's best for you. If not worrying about your brother will make you happier, then as your friend, it's my obligation to see that your mind is clear."

"*My friend.* That's one way of putting it! What friend throws another on a plane and just waltzes them across the Atlantic?" Anger replaced my embarrassment.

His look turned to one of utter frustration. "You know why I had to do what I did."

"Look. We can talk until we're blue in the face, but a fact is a fact. And besides, there's no time for this. You have a festival to open."

"Your needs will always come first."

"Before those of the Tribunal and your clan? Really?" I asked in my most skeptical tone. Obviously, they could not.

He was about to answer when a voice shouted from a short distance away, interrupting.

Chapter Seventeen

Mira

"Calan, we need you. Now, bro," Logan called out.

"We're not finished here," Calan warned.

I shrugged, not convinced as we hustled to join the others. He left to join his brothers while I squeezed between other attendees to get closer to the stage. When the opening ceremony began, Sherry appeared at my side, looking pleased with herself. "Glad you could join us."

"Wouldn't miss it for the world." *Like I have a choice.* Then I remembered what Lachlan had said. "Thanks for arranging for a session with the seer."

She rubbed her hands together with glee. "You are *so* going to enjoy it. An appointment with the Soothsayer of Lochness is much sought after in these parts." She glanced at her phone. "And yours is in fifteen minutes, as soon as this is over." She nodded at the brothers now congregated on the dais.

The wooden platform was situated about three feet above the ground and was festooned with a large banner announcing the Spirit of Creigbourne festival. The brothers were lined up with microphones in hand. *Awesome sight.* All three were now in traditional kilts, their snowy white shirt fronts exposing their superior builds. With all their hair tied back, exposing how similar their facial features were with their slashes of cheekbones and generous full lips, it was hard not to imagine a bevy of women throwing themselves at their feet, especially with those arresting green-colored eyes. I shook my head to dispel the image. I was a woman of logic and science, not a damn groupie.

"Welcome to all the lads and lassies present today for the one hundredth and fifty-year anniversary of the first Spirit of Creigbourne festival. We are honored and pleased to stand before you to announce that this year we have even more people in attendance than ever before."

"They make quite a sight, the brothers," Sherry said, her eyes shining with interest.

She sounded besotted to me and I pursed my lips.

"What? You don't agree?" she asked, her reddish-colored eyebrows rising.

"I'll admit they grow them huge in the Highlands."

"They *are* well built, all over if you know what I mean," Sherry said with a smug smile on her lips as if she knew a secret.

Ugh. Wait a damn minute, was she suggesting that she and Calan had gone to bed? Before I could question her, the sound of loud applause interrupted. I had missed the end of the speech.

"Great! Let's get you over to the standing stones. Time for you to discover something important about your future." Before I could protest, Sherry was busy pushing people aside to hustle through the crowd.

The elder woman, her bony hands outstretched toward the sky, was a sight to behold, especially with long thick strands of white hair fluttering in the breeze. Was it posturing, or something more? With my interest piqued, I allowed her grandniece to drag me the last few steps toward her. Was it going to happen out in the open? I'd rather hoped for a private meeting, not wanting the whole world to know what she was going to say.

"Grandmother, Soothsayer of Creigbourne, this is Mira Tala, the woman I told you about." Sherry sounded breathless, like she was as excited as me. Why was she taking such an interest? Just because I offered her a compliment or two? It seemed a bit over the top, though perhaps this was just her way.

But something told me to stay on guard. After all, her cousin had tossed me on his private jet. Who knew what Sherry was up to? She did seem to fancy Calan. Perhaps she bribed the old woman to say something to derail us? The thought made me stop and think. Did I want to see where a relationship with Calan could lead? *Maybe.* He did have some wonderful qualities aside from thinking he knew what was good for me. Flash bulletin—*I know best what's good for me, Mr. Calan Creig.*

I forced myself to remain in the present, taking the offered hand. What was I supposed to call her?

"Hello, ma'am," I said, not wanting to say the wrong thing.

Her bright green eyes, surprisingly not faded with age, bore into mine, surrounded by a myriad of wrinkles that added a soulfulness to her appearance. A vast ocean of knowledge lurked in their depths, making me wish to learn more. Our world was so full of miracles, such amazing creatures roaming the land and swimming in the ocean, that if only we stopped for just a moment and absorbed how lucky we were to be a part of it, even if for such a brief moment of time, we'd probably treat it better. Or maybe that was the point, that time was so short and precious that we were nonstop in our hopes of outrunning it. I shook my head. If this elderly woman could bring out such deep thoughts just by the mere fact of her presence, what else lurked for me to absorb and understand?

"Ah, Miracle Camile Tala. Good that you're here. Come. We need to speak alone."

Good. Private was best. I dutifully followed her to an unimposing structure set discreetly to the side of the imposing standing stones.

"Sit," she instructed. There were only two straight-backed chairs set around a small round table maybe eighteen inches in diameter in the center of the space. The inside of the tent was dim, lit only by the light shining forth from a crystal ball perched on the tabletop, which seemed a rather hokey thing for her to have if she was a real seer. I'd have thought she'd be a water scryer or just take my hands and read the energy that existed in all things. The atmosphere was warmer than outside, cozier, but also a bit intimidating. I was at the disadvantage in here and the old woman had all the control. What would she share?

I took my seat across from her, reminding myself to relax, to drop my shoulders, that this was meant to be enlightening, not intimidating.

"The light is only for focus," she said, as if she were used to people questioning its existence.

"Of course," I murmured, waiting for her to begin the reading.

"Please, take my hands."

So, she did read energy.

I did as she requested, finding hers cool and dry, the skin paper thin, the fingers slightly twisted at the joints. Careful to not squeeze too hard in case she had painful arthritis, I waited while she closed her eyes and remained quiet. Uncomfortable with the growing silence, I stirred in my chair.

Her eyes sprang open and instead of the normal bright green, they appeared opaque as if cataracts had developed in the past few minutes. Was it a trick?

"Your brother needs you. He's in trouble. You must go home."

Shocked, I sat unmoving, trying to make sense of her words. I'd thought she would be saying something about my love life or such, not give such a direct message of doom and gloom.

"My brother? What do you know? Where is he?"

She stared unblinking at me. "He's in a dark place in the land of desert and sage. He's asking for you, hiding out."

That didn't help much. All this I already knew. To find him I would need much more than vague references. I knew this because it wasn't like I hadn't tried to find my brother when he'd just upped and disappeared before. The first time I had even gone to the cops only to get blasted by Evan when he showed up a few days later. He liked to live under the radar, come and go as he pleased.

"What else can you see?" I asked in frustration. "Evan's in trouble, that I already know. But searching the streets of Vegas to find him would take forever without more of a lead. I know—I've done it before with zero results."

But anything she could share might actually help a private investigator like Calan suggested he wanted to hire. I desperately wanted to find my brother—who wouldn't?—but I needed more than this vague warning. I knew more about this already than the seer knew. That was obvious.

The woman shrugged. "The goddess only gives what she gives. It is up to us to act. You have been warned."

"Anything about my love life?" I asked eagerly, trying to shift her focus to learn something else before our time was up.

She shook her head, her long locks trailing around her like seaweed though the way she pressed her lips together made me feel she was holding something back, not wanting to speak. I found that strange. And very disappointing.

She closed her eyes again for a few seconds, and when she opened the lids to reveal her irises, they had cleared, the green shining like shimmering, shifting pools of deep water. *Green eyes.* Most people I had met since coming to the Highlands of Scotland had similar green eyes. Perhaps that was one of the clues to who was and who wasn't a werewolf? A solid piece of evidence would be highly appreciated. The urge to study and learn more bore down on me. I was in the land of the supernatural—surely I could learn more here than anywhere? But my disquiet about Evan grew. Yes, a part of me did want to head back to the states as soon as possible, not that I could find him on my own. But leaving right now seemed premature, with all I could learn right here.

"Will you go now? Search for your brother?" the old woman pressed, holding on to me tighter.

I pulled my fingers from her steely grasp. She had strength in those hands, almost shockingly so.

"I don't know." It was best to be honest. After all, what was it really to her? Sure, she'd tried to be helpful, but vague references only upset a person and weren't all that helpful. It wasn't my first rodeo and I wasn't one to run around willy-nilly. I needed time to assess this, perhaps talk to Calan about it? He'd had my back a few times on things happening in the past few days, and so far, other than my ending up in Scotland, had proved his worth. Actually, sitting here and thinking of him, I found myself almost smiling at some of the things we'd shared. And there'd been enough damn excitement to last a lifetime.

"Don't leave it too long. Evan needs you, his only living relative."

"How did you know that?" I asked. *A rather useless bit of information. Now Evan's actual address, that would be what the goddess should reveal.*

"The goddess reveals what she reveals." The woman's expression was so neutral I found it annoying now. Fat lot I had learned from the famous Soothsayer of Lochness.

"Well, next time you speak to her, let her know that more specifics would be helpful."

"You think to disparage the goddess?"

Ah, so she did care about something under all that superior guise. Hiding my smile, I got to my feet as gracefully as I could manage with one of them suffering from pins and needles from the overly upright positioning of the chair. How did the old lady manage?

"No. But I have to say she could be more useful. Thank you for your time and I wish you good day."

I felt her eyes boring into me as I hurried from the claustrophobic enclosure, happy to be breathing fresh air after the stuffiness of the tent.

"Mira. What did my grandmother have to say?" Sherry hurried over to ask, her face shining with expectation.

I shrugged. "Not much."

"Oh. I thought she'd have a lot to tell you." Sherry pressed her lips together, her eyes expressing disappointment.

"No, I guess the goddess wasn't up for too much chitchat this early in the morning," I said, half-joking.

The young woman looked around, then leaned in closer like a fellow conspirator. "If you need to go home, I can help you. I can get you on a plane in no time."

My eyes flew open at the revelation and something clicked in my brain. Was Sherry behind the old woman's warning? Would they be this devious? I shook my head. Surely not. I must be imagining things. Everyone else had spoken highly of her grandmother's abilities. She was famous for it.

"Thanks, but that won't be necessary. Calan is dealing with things for me."

"Calan? What do you mean?" she asked, her gaze sharpening.

"My brother Evan has left home again and he's going to help me find him. Hire someone. But thanks for offering."

"You should come by my spa later. Get the works on me. It might be fun to have some girl time," Sherry said.

"Maybe. We'll see." I was rather more interested to spending time with Calan. I missed him, his dry wit and his protectiveness, though a bit extreme, at least meant he cared.

"What? You have too much to do on holiday that you can't even take some time to relax properly?" she teased, linking her arm through mine. "Come. At least let me buy you a drink. Something to take the edge off. I know grandmother can be rather taxing. But have you met The Creig?" She rolled her eyes.

She was just trying to be friendly after all and she certainly did not know the real deal, that this was hardly a holiday but something else entirely. Well, I was confused now as to what this was. A short break to hide out from the bad guys, a time to get to know an intriguing man better, or a chance to get to learn more about Wulvers? *Might as well add a mini-vacation while we're at it.*

"Okay. Set up something for late afternoon. I can at least take a tour of this spa of yours."

"Great! Now let's try some of that sparkling apple cider that my Aunt Jean is always handing out free samples of to her favorite niece."

Not a half-dozen steps later and Calan stood in our path. "I need to borrow Mira. If you'll excuse us." It was not a request but an order. I didn't appreciate how easily he was dismissing Sherry.

I squinted at the ridiculously handsome man in the kilt and held onto Sherry's arm. She had gone still at my side. I sensed this exchange had hurt her feelings and I was having none of that. The woman had been trying to be nice to me. "My friend and I are about to partake of some refreshments. Perhaps you'd like to join us?"

"I have news of Evan."

My eyes widened. "Why didn't you say so? Excuse me, Sherry, I really do need to hear this." I pulled away from her and grabbed Calan's shirt front. "Spill."

"He's in Vegas."

"Just like she said," I murmured, watching Sherry walk away from us through the milling crowd before vanishing from view. I felt bad for ditching her so quickly, but the chance at some news about my brother loomed much larger than spending time enjoying myself. Besides, we'd catch up later at the spa.

"Who?"

"Doesn't matter. Where in Vegas exactly? Is he okay?"

"Yes, he's fine. My guy tracked him down to a small rundown hotel on the outskirts of town."

"Like the Bluebird?" I asked, suddenly very aware of events we'd shared in that intimate setting. Truthfully, events I wouldn't mind repeating and often.

"Not quite as nice. The Bluebird will be forever ingrained on my mind as a great place for new beginnings," he teased, his full lips curving up and making me want to taste them again. I swallowed, making myself focus on the present.

"When do we leave?"

When he remained silent, I glanced up at him again. His eyes bore into mine. What was he thinking?

"I need to go *now,*" I said, grabbing his arm to make him see how urgent it was.

"Not until we come to an agreement. I need to give the Tribunal an answer to this situation and time is running out. They are not known for their patience." He took a deep breath, expanding those awesome lungs of his.

Could he be better built? *I think not.*

"Come. Let's talk." Calan tugged me along and made our way to the outskirts of the crowd, then to an even more secluded spot shrouded by a canopy of leafy trees.

"Okay. I'll give you my take on all this. But I need you to listen and not interrupt. Can you do that?"

I nodded, pretending to zip my mouth shut.

"I've decided to take the fall for this."

"What?"

"You promised," he said, arching his eyebrows at me.

I nodded. "Go on. Lay out your plan."

"I'm going to pretend that it was me that got careless, exposed us—"

"They'll never believe that for one second."

He gave me a stoic look. "They will if I sell it properly. I will have to resign my commission, of course. In return, you must destroy all the evidence you have collected."

I frowned. "That doesn't seem right at all. You didn't do anything wrong. Well, other than throw me on a plane and haul my ass to Scotland. However, I now know why you did it and hold no animosity for it. Or at least I'm trying not to."

I tried to smile but his words worried me. This whole thing felt wrong. Why should he give up on his dreams, his life's work to cover my ass? We should be able to figure a way through this where neither of us lost, but I just couldn't see what that was yet.

"Why would you do that for me? You could just throw me to the wolves." At his look, I corrected myself. "Okay, poor choice of words, but you know what I mean. This isn't right."

"I would do anything for you, Mira, surely you know that by now? I know we only met a few days ago, but to me it feels like you've always been in my life. That it was just a matter of time before we were fated to meet, you and I."

I ignored how hopeful his words made me, how a part of me was beginning to feel the same. To think a man like Calan wanted to spend time with me. But none of this changed the fact that I still wanted with every bit of my fiber to become famous for the person who discovered something important, be somebody. Confused more than ever, feeling pushed against the wall, I was at a loss to know what to say or do next. Was I not the person I thought I was? Was my need to make something of myself adding blinders to my thoughts? Uneasy, I sought the best answer I could manage.

"Can I give you my answer later? It's so much to take in. I just need time to process it all."

"Of course." His eyes shadowed with a new emotion. Was that hurt? I couldn't imagine Mr. McHottie being hurt by a woman. He was just too alpha, too sure of himself.

"Would you like to tour the fair?" he asked.

His posture had changed. *Back to being Mr. Enigmatic.* Why was taking time to think things through not considered the norm? All my life I had learned to be extra careful because something bad could be lurking around the next corner. It took real courage to do what I was doing, trying to discover more of the secrets of the world without being crushed. Maybe I was a teensy bit more afraid of giving my heart than anything? People always seemed to be leaving me. First my father, then my mother and brother, and now if I didn't do what Calan wanted, I sensed he too might just abandon me to those in power that could squash me like a bug.

No. That wasn't a fair assessment. He was trying to help me. He could have just handed me over to the Tribunal without another word. Instead, he too was taking chances.

"I would like that," I said, slipping my hand through his arm and giving him a big smile.

His eyes widened with appreciation. "You should smile more, *thasgaidh.*"

"What does that word mean?" I hadn't had the opportunity to look it up.

"My darling."

"Nice." I caught sight of Sherry watching us from a side kiosk, holding a mug of something that steamed in the open air. She wasn't smiling.

I waved, thinking she might not have seen me, but she turned away before I could nab her attention. Oh well, I'd catch up with her later.

"Say, there's a game of chance," I said spotting a booth that promised a stuffed toy unicorn for hitting a target with a water pistol. "I love unicorns!"

"Then my lady shall have one."

Chapter Eighteen

Calan

Progress. Finally. For the first time Mira and I were experiencing some normalcy or at least as much as could be offered in extraordinary times, not racing around Vegas with the bloodhounds on our heels. She needed this time with things not so out of kilter, more in alignment, so I forced down the instant urge to make her mine in all ways, instead focusing on gaining her trust.

"Step right up and gain the lady a unique unicorn to remember this day for years to come," the barker announced, an expansive look on his face. I knew the man well enough—he'd stepped in to cover the booth when a stomach bug had overtaken a few of the vendors.

I winked at him now. "I'll take one of those pistols and gain this beauty a fitting prize. A one-of-a-kind gift for a one-of-a-kind woman."

Within thirty seconds I had won Mira the unicorn of her choice. When I presented it to her, the grin that covered her beautiful face touched my heart in a new way. A lifetime spent with this woman lay ahead of me and I itched to just get at it. To have a handholding and commit to her being my Forever Mate in front of the whole community. The urge to rush her to a decision rose again, but I thrust it aside. Just give her—no, make that us—this day, then I'd turn myself in as the culprit behind this. My mind spun with ways of how to spin the situation just right to get the Tribunal to believe me.

"I need to find the ladies' room," Mira said, hugging the huge unicorn close to her chest.

"Over there," I said, pointing at the small pavilion that held the facilities.

She leaned in and kissed my cheek. "Thanks for Billy."

"Billy the unicorn?" I asked, shaking my head at the fun bit of nonsense. "Sounds like a children's book."

"I always wanted to write and illustrate children's books," she said in tone of voice filled with enthusiasm and awe. "Especially about a mythical creature. Think of all the adventures that could happen!"

"You should do that," I said with even more enthusiasm than Mira. Was this a way forward for us? A chance for her to be known worldwide for something that would bring happiness to children. Hell, I'd buy the best publisher on the planet and begin that process in a heartbeat. "I want to help make that dream come true. Will you let me, *thasgaidh?* It would mean the world to me if you'd let me do this for you."

Her eyes lit up with such power I could but stare. I tenderly reached out and caressed the side of her face, the skin so velvety. "Are we going into business together?"

"Yes! Let's do this thing! And now I really need to use the ladies' room."

She danced off and turned to wave just as she made it to the edge of the building, then vanished from view. My pulse sped up. This was it, our way forward. Just one last hurdle with the Tribunal and everything was a go.

I stood and watched the fair-goers, breathing easier now, certain the air had never smelled as sweet. The minutes ticked by and still no Mira, though I kept checking out the doorway she should emerge from. What was keeping her?

My cell rang, distracting me. I checked the number. *Damn.* The Tribunal. I just wanted one day of peace. Was it too much to ask?

A terrible scream rent the perfect calm of the morn. My blood running cold, I raced toward the building Mira had entered, certain the piercing ongoing screams and shouts for help were coming from there.

"What is it? What's wrong?" I yelled at the woman standing in the doorway of the ladies' bathroom.

She turned eyes widened by fear at me. "Someone's been attacked by a wolf. I interrupted them, hit that horrible creature with my taser. It's gone, but the poor woman. So much blood..." She stood frozen and I had to make my way around her, only to be hit with an image that would brand my mind forever more.

Mira. She lay on the floor, still as death, blood pooling around her.

I raced to her side, pulling her into my arms. Her eyelids fluttered and my heart started again.

"Mira, speak to me. Are you okay? Who did this to you?"

Her expression remained confused as she looked into my eyes. The pain I could see in their depths made me want to crush whoever was responsible for this. I began checking her out to see where the blood was coming from. Her shoulder, just below the carotid artery. *Wolf bite.* My anger exploded in my chest. Who could have done this? She was bleeding but it was slowing down. Thank God the bite hadn't been an inch to the left.

"I don't know. A wolf…it sprung at me…sorry. That woman…" she raised her arm to point at the woman still standing in the doorway. "Where's Billy?"

"I don't know." Her toy was the last thing on my mind.

"Please. Look. He means a lot to me. The future."

I glanced around and spotted the errant unicorn undamaged in a corner. The woman in the doorway scrambled to retrieve Billy and stood holding it so that Mira could see him.

"He's right here, *thasgaidh*. You need a doctor. I'm not sure if I should move you or not." I pulled out my cell phone and made the call to one of the doctors always on standby for The Creig. She had round-the-clock care to be certain of help when needed.

In less than a minute, one arrived.

"Dr. MacDonald, this is Mira. She was just attacked by a wolf," I said, moving enough so that the medical man could crouch down and inspect Mira.

"Can you move your arms and legs?" he asked.

She nodded and complied.

"We need to get you inside. I think she's fine…if you would just carry her, Calan?"

I quickly picked her up, being gentle as possible, then strode out of the bathroom and down the path toward our ancestral home. Dr. MacDonald and the woman who had found Mira trailed behind us.

"What's happened? What's going on?"

All around us voices were asking. I didn't stop for a second but kept marching. Everybody could wait until my mate was taken care of. Nothing else mattered.

I lay her tenderly on a padded table in the small onsite infirmary and stepped back just enough for the doctor to help her. He cleaned the wound and put in a few stitches.

"I can't guarantee she won't carry a scar, but I've made them as tiny as possible." He applied a dressing over the area. "I'm going to give her a shot of antibiotics to prevent infection."

Infection.

The full horror of what had just occurred washed over me. Mira was now in certainty of becoming a werewolf by the next full moon. It could only have been one of ours that had bitten her, because no other wolf would dare transgress onto our land.

A new terror rose. What if she didn't survive the change? Not all humans did. Then I remembered the recent finding of the Lupus Sanguis Chalice and I breathed a little easier. If necessary, I would send for it. I'd pay a king's ransom for its use but no one ever had to pay money to have it available to them. It was loaned out to whoever needed it. But it was obvious from the bite and the fact that the attack had been interrupted that this had been meant to be a death attack and nothing else.

The woman who had tasered the beast was still in the room, clinging onto the unicorn. I got to my feet and went to thank her, although it was hardly enough. I would have to come up with something far bigger to express my gratitude.

"Thank you." I took the unicorn from the woman, who was a bit older than I had first realized. "Your name?"

"Joan Aiken. I'm one of the vendors. I run Sweet Heaven Bakery with my daughter, Jennifer." She held out her hand.

"I'm—"

"I know who you are. Everyone does. Nice to make your acquaintance, Calan Creig."

"Anything you need, you just ask. You saved my mate's life today."

Her eyes widened. "Are you saying what I think you're saying? You're off the market, Calan? My daughter's going to be so disappointed." She put a hand over her mouth at what had spilled out.

"I need to promise you to secrecy until I've had the time to announce it. Can you do that?"

"Of course. Just glad I could help." She shook her head. "Such a beauty. Who could have done such a thing to her?"

"I don't know but I intend to find out." I prayed that the scent I had caught a whiff of in the bathroom wasn't the one who had attempted to murder Mira. Surely it was just a coincidence, that they'd just gone into the bathroom moments before the attack? But I needed to check that lead out. Maybe they'd seen something.

"Anything else you remember, Joan? Did you recognize the animal?"

She shook her head. "It all happened so fast. A blur of movement, then the animal running away when I entered the room, its mouth dripping blood." The woman turned paler and her eyes held real fear. "Do I need to warn the others? Is a rogue wolf loose in the fair? That hardly seems likely, but maybe?"

"I don't think so. I believe Mira was targeted by one of our own. Someone lay in wait and took the opportunity to do this horrid thing." I raked a hand through my hair, tugging out the band that held it in place. "But to be on the safe side, we'll be announcing that the venue will be shut down for the rest of the day." I pulled my hair into a tighter fistful and refastened it. *Time to go to work.*

"I'll go shut down my booth. Get my daughter home."

"Good. I'll handle the rest."

Joan left and I went to Mira's side. "I'm going to take care of this. The doctor will stay with you. Keep the doors locked and don't let anyone in. I'll send a couple of security guards. You okay with that, Dr. MacDonald?"

"Of course." The man nodded.

I kissed Mira on the forehead. She grabbed at my arm, her expression worried. "Be careful, Calan. That wolf is dangerous."

"I will, *thasgaidh.*"

"I like the sound of your voice when you say that word of endearment. Like I'm somebody important."

She let go of me and I gave her a smile of encouragement. Though the urge to track down the beast was firing up my blood, reassuring my mate was of even more importance.

"Get used to it. I intend to use it often because you are somebody of incalculable importance to me."

"Incalculable, eh?" she teased. "That sounds nice. Never been that important to anyone before." Her eyes were glazed from the painkillers the doctor had administered, her words slowing.

"Get used to it. You are all that and more, *thasgaidh*."

I hurried to leave now, impatient to get to Mira's attacker and take them down. Not until then would I rest.

Exiting the castle, I discovered a frenzy of activity. Word had spread and people were packing up. Lachlan strode over, his expression dark.

"What's happened? I heard Mira was attacked?"

"Yes. I'm on it."

"Who was it?" my brother demanded, striding along at my side as we hurried through the crowd.

"One of ours. I need to speak with our cousin Sherry. I caught a whiff of her scent in the bathroom where Mira was found."

"You think it was Sherry?" Lachlan's expression was skeptical.

"I don't know. But she was there around that time. Maybe she saw something? Anyway, we need to find her. Discover what she knows."

"Yes, of course."

"When was the last time you saw her?" I asked.

"Not for a while. Maybe she left for the spa?" Lachlan said, his eyes scanning the crowd.

Frustrated that we couldn't spot her anywhere, I made a decision. "I need to shift and track that scent."

"Wait until everyone leaves. Otherwise, you might get shot. Everyone's agitated."

"Right." I pulled out my cell phone and called the spa.

"Sherry there?" I barked into the phone.

"Sorry, no. Do you want to leave a message?"

I disconnected the call. "Not there. Where else could she be?"

"Let's put the word out. And announce it over the intercom system," Lachlan suggested.

"Good. Do that and I'll check with some of the vendors that she deals with."

Fifteen minutes later and I still had no idea where our cousin had gotten to. It might have been innocent, or it might not have been. But needing to know was eating at my stomach lining. The crowd had mostly dispersed. Lachlan reappeared at my side, shaking his head to let me know no one had seen her.

"I can't wait any longer. I need to track now before the scent is completely gone."

"Should be safe enough. Let's start at the bathroom. We'll team it."

Logan came hurrying up at that moment. "What's the plan?"

As soon as I explained, he was in on it.

"Okay, we start over there." I pointed out the pavilion that housed the bathrooms.

The three of us shifted and stalked up to the doorway. Pushing it open with a front paw, I prowled the inside of the room. Yes. Sherry's scent was the strongest, indicating she could have well have shifted to her wolf form while inside. But why? It made no sense for her to attack Mira. Or did it? I thought back to the numerous times she'd hinted at us hooking up. Was this a simple case of jealousy? The thought sickened me and made me reassess how to handle the situation.

I took off at a quick trot to follow the scent trail, my brothers flanking my sides. Wulver Cave seemed to be the location the wolf was headed. Why trap themselves there? I would have thought a wolf in such deep trouble would have thought to leave the island as quickly a possible, not hang around to be dealt with.

"Stay on guard. This could be a trap."

In tight formation we crossed the final stretch of land that led to the cave, the scent growing stronger with each step.

Then Sherry came into view at the top of the rise, still in wolf form, standing tall and defiant, blood still anointing her muzzle.

I needed to know why she'd committed the horrific deed more than anything.

"I'm shifting back to human. I need to speak with her."

Before my brothers could object, I was through the dimension that allowed energy transfers and back as human. Ignoring my naked state, I stood before her and spoke. "Why did you do it, Sherry?"

She too had shifted, though she looked no less defiant, her arms crossed over her chest. "You know why. I did us all a favor. She was going to expose us, make us all scientific experiments. Ruin all our lives. Did you want that? She didn't care about us, only about being famous and gaining that by using our clan. She disgusts me."

"Who told you about Mira?"

"Most of us know. It's not like it's something you can hide. And to think an alpha like you has to kowtow to that bitch. In the old days she'd be caged and given a death sentence. Things are no different now, not if protecting your clan still matters to you?"

Her words hit hard and it was all I could do not to strike back.

"I had it all under control. She's not going to reveal our existence."

"You sure about that?"

"Yes. Mira and I are Forever Mates. You can't change that. And now she's going to become one of us. Your attack didn't work. She's going to recover."

"I was interrupted by that woman. Otherwise, you'd be out one Forever Mate."

I was suddenly being held back by my two brothers, who stopped me from doing what I wanted to do. I shook my head, stunned things had taken such a left turn.

A part of me understood what Sherry had done. It was in our honor code, never revealing who we are. But it was not her place to do what she'd done. It was mine. And I had been blinded by my lust for Mira. And now I loved her, through and through. I had been so close to convincing her to abandon using us to make herself famous in her field. Now she was about to become one of us. What would she do now? Exposing us was to expose herself. Did her need to become famous reach that far?

God, please don't let that be the case.

Chapter Nineteen

Mira

I awoke with a start, sensing someone in the room with me. Fear struck. Was it that wolf from earlier?

My vision cleared and I groaned when I saw who was sitting at my bedside. The Creig. She looked quite official, dressed in a stiff black dress that brought out the matriarch in her to a tee. Maybe the tiara was a bit much? But still, she looked the part.

"Seems my grandson has taken a liking to ye. I do want to say that I'm sorry for the way things turned out. I would have seen ye turned over to the Tribunal, not attacked. Violence cannot be condoned, even if it's understandable."

Comforting words. I took a deep breath, tamping down my urge to scream. It was best to suck it up and explain. "I've gotten to know some of the clan members and I'm seeing things differently now. I like what you all have. A close-knit community is so amazing in this time and space when people seem to abandon others with way too much ease. I care about all of you now and I don't want to see anyone hurt."

"So ye will abandon your plans to destroy all we have built?"

"I wouldn't paint such a dark, devious plan on my side. I just wanted to make something of myself in this world." Even as I said it, I winced.

"And now you feel differently?"

I wanted to share how I felt with Calan first, so I hedged my words. "Calan is an amazing man. And I know I like most of you in this clan that I've met since I've arrived." I couldn't help the last part. I mean, the woman was tough, but she was telling it like she saw it. I should be allowed the same right.

"I grow on people, once they get to know me."

Was that a twinkle in her eye? I stared at her, wondering if it had been a trick of the light.

She patted my hand that rested on the blanket someone had pulled over me. "I am pleased that ye have come to yer senses, Mira."

Even though I hadn't actually said that things would be different going ahead, she seemed to assume so. Did that mean I was just expected to surrender all that I wanted in this life? Conflicted by her casual attitude to what I would be giving up by just abandoning any hope of being important in my field, I pressed my lips together to stop myself from revealing more.

"Now, I will leave ye to rest. Soon the change will come, and I pray it turns out well. My grandson needs for that to happen as well."

"What do you mean? The change?"

But the elderly woman forewent answering my query and got to her feet, making her way stiffly from the infirmary, her back ramrod straight. The doctor must have been hovering outside in the hallway, because he came right in to check on me.

"How are you feeling, Mira?" Dr. MacDonald asked. He appeared to be mid-thirties, not as large as the Creig brothers, but sturdy and well built.

"Better thanks. Now what happens?"

"How do you mean?"

"Will I be further affected by being wolf bit? I mean, there are legends about what happens after being bitten by a wolf, like turning into one at the next full moon," I joked, hedging my words, not certain if he was one, though it seemed likely since he worked so closely with them. Seemed I had more to worry about now than just publishing a paper on the existence of a species. A *lot* more if the stories about how to become a werewolf were true.

"What do you know about the Creig clan?" he asked, his green eyes serious and penetrating. *Those green eyes again.*

"I know one of their well-hidden secrets," I said, still being careful.

"I see. Well, I think you should talk to Calan first. Then we can have a talk." His words were meant kindly and I relaxed somewhat.

He checked my vitals. "You're doing better, though your blood pressure is high. Try to relax more and drink more fluids."

Weird. I normally had low blood pressure. Did the higher reading mean something more sinister was up with my system or was it just a result of today's attack? I still had the jitters so maybe that was it?

I drank a glass of water and lay back on the bed, pulling the cover to my chin. But the longer I remained still, the more antsy I became. Finally, I threw back the blanket and got to my feet, disgusted with my inability to rest. I needed to get out of here, walk it off.

Opening the infirmary door, I ran smack into one of the guards who had been posted outside.

"Excuse me, miss, but I don't think—" He put up a hand to stop me but I eluded him and kept on walking.

"I'm fine," I hollered over my shoulder. "I need to take a walk."

I strode down the long hallway and began looking for my room. I needed a shower in the worst way and clean clothes.

"Can I help you?" The guard had caught up with me, his expression dead serious.

"I'm looking for my suite. I need to clean up." This place was just too damn big.

He pulled out his cell phone and made a quick call.

"Okay, I'll take you there. But be warned, I've been ordered to stay with you. I'll be right outside your door if you need anything."

"Fine." I conceded the need for the heightened security, vanishing into my bedroom as soon as he pointed it out. A quick shower and a change of clothes were in order. Entering the bathroom, my appearance stunned me. My God, but I was a mess. Blood soaked my dress and stained my skin. I tore off the ruined garment and my underwear in a fit of temper and climbed into the shower.

Ah, the warmth of the rain shower seeped into my pores, renewing my equilibrium. My shoulder stung like hell where the doctor had stitched me up, but I stood and let the sense of renewal continue for long moments before shampooing my hair and soaping my body. Drying off, I wrapped a towel around my hair and hurried to find something soft and comfortable to wear for a stroll. Or maybe a run.

Dressed in yoga pants and a matching zippered top with no time to question the urgent need to keep moving, I raced past the security guard without giving him a second glance. I did sense him right behind me but kept up the steady pace out onto the lawn. *Ah, fresh air.* I took in huge gulps of it, my heart racing. Something was up with my body, but I ignored the warning.

"Maybe you could give a guy a break, miss, stay close to the castle?"

Not ready to concede an inch, I spared the man a glance, then experienced a moment of pity for the worried look in his eyes. "I need to work something out and moving is my way of getting there." I had run from the pain of my brother leaving me in hot water. Then the betrayal of my best friend. Now this. Being bitten by a wolf. *What am I? A calamity magnet?*

"I'll stay where you can see me. Run laps around the yard."

He looked relieved and spoke into the device fastened to his shoulder like the cops back home, to share my whereabouts with his team, I imagined.

I began to run laps, keeping a sharp eye out for company. A sudden thought hit, making me scramble to remember. What part of the moon cycle were we in at the moment? *Oh. Shit.* I scanned the horizon to the east of the castle as realization hit me like a ten-ton truck. In a few hours, the full moon would be rising right over there. What did it mean for me? I needed to talk to Calan in the worst way.

Where was he? The urge to stop running in a useless circle began to eat at me. I wanted to take a hard right and head out into the wilds of the Highlands, find Calan and confront him with my questions.

I was about to break my word to the security guard when I caught sight of three wolves coming over a rise in the land, backlit by the sun, their green eyes glinting in the distance. I used my hand to shield my eyes, my heart beating like a drum. Was I about to be attacked again?

At that same moment the security guard took notice of the scenario and began to cross the distance between us, his steps quickly turning into a fast clip. Was he also worried? And more importantly, would he arrive in time?

About to turn on my heel and head in the opposite direction, I waited a split second longer. Maybe running would just draw more attention to me. This was why I needed to speak with Calan. *Find out what the hell I'm facing.*

The security guard put up a hand as if to stop me. *Don't worry, I'm not about to attack anyone, buddy.* Half out of breath he announced, "It's okay. These are friendlies."

Friendlies. Just exactly how friendly were we talking?

Then three naked brothers were advancing toward me and I was too stunned to move. *Holy shit! What a sight!* Big, beautiful men, naked and in the prime of youth. I could not imagine a more impressive sight. Lachlan and Logan veered off, and Calan kept coming toward me.

Well, this was one thing it wouldn't be too hard to get used to in this new existence. I couldn't imagine seeing wolves morph into gorgeous naked men would ever get old.

"What happened?" I asked, soon as Calan was close enough to ask. "Where did you go?"

"What are you doing out here?" he frowned. "You should be resting. The full moon's rising in a few hours."

"About that," I said, trying not to salivate at his nakedness. I adverted my eyes. God, I just wanted to jump his bones. What was stopping me? Oh yeah, my totally messed-up life that I needed answers to. "What's going on? I need to know everything like yesterday."

"I need to get dressed. Come. We'll talk inside."

I dutifully followed him, filled with such overwhelming feelings of lust and longing that I was about to burst at the seams. I noted how much better I felt, like brand-new strength was pouring into every muscle and bone in my body by the minute. *Ironwoman, that's me.*

Inside the back door, Calan pulled on a pair of pants and a shirt, and, barefoot, pulled me along behind him and behind the first door we came to. *A sitting room, by the looks of it.* We sat on a sofa and faced each other.

"Okay, spill."

"What are your intentions, Mira? About keeping our clan's secret?"

I swallowed. *This again.* "Okay, I've put a moratorium on that question for the moment. First, I need to know what's going to happen to me?"

He frowned. "What happens to you is directly related to my question."

"You mean if I don't agree to keep silent, something bad is going to happen to me?" I squinted my eyes at him.

"I'm here for you, to protect you, even if just from yourself and any bad decision you make."

"Bad? It's my life, Calan. I'll live it as I see fit!"

"So you intend to expose us?"

The look in his eyes scared me, though I knew instinctively that he would never harm me.

"Yes, no, maybe? I mean some of you are dangerous. Maybe the world needs to know that to keep themselves safe. But you're not telling me what I need to know and the moon will be rising soon. Am I going to be okay? What's going to happen?"

"You will undergo the change tonight."

"Become a wolf? Is it painful?"

He shook his head. "No, but for some, it's dangerous. We have no idea how it will be for you. But I've never seen anyone look so strong after being bitten. Normally they fall ill, sometimes for days on end."

He looked thoughtful while his words gave me hope that I'd not lose the high I was currently experiencing.

"Who did this to me? One of your clan?"

He nodded, his eyes tormented by something. "Yes, Sherry, my cousin. She thought she was doing the right thing by taking you out and eliminating the threat to us."

"You condone that?"

"No, but I understand it. But I also hate that you were harmed in the process."

He glanced at the dressing covering my wound and my memory of the attack rose up. I forced it away with extreme prejudice. I was not going to allow myself to appear weak.

"Where's Sherry now?"

"We dealt with her. She won't bother you again."

"How?" I didn't want to see anyone harmed on my account. I had liked the woman and especially the fact she was a business owner.

When he didn't answer straight away, I spoke up. "What do we do now?"

"I need to report to the Tribunal. Time's run out, Mira. The piper always has to be paid." The stony look in his green eyes, turning them to crystal with no way for me to see into their normally liquid depths, made me pause. What was he going to do? I felt shut out and I hated the sensation.

"What does that mean exactly? What's the plan?"

He looked away from me. "An alpha does what he must."

"I want to be there. I have just as much a stake in it as you do."

"Absolutely not!"

Never had I seen him so adamant. Where had the negotiator gone?

His phone dinged and he glanced at the text. He continued staring at the screen with such focus that I knew something huge was up.

"What is it? What's wrong?"

"This is going to be hard for you to hear." His warning gave me pause.

"Is it Evan? Is he okay?" I should have insisted on going to Vegas before this, seen with my own eyes that my brother was fine, not take someone else's word for it.

"No, not your brother. It's about your father."

"*Deadbeat?* What about him?"

"He lived in Alaska after he left your mother, off-grid."

"Alaska. That's a hell of a long ways from Vegas. What was he doing up there? Gold mining?" I said with extreme prejudice. I was entitled to be a bit ornery since he'd left us high and dry.

"No, but he used to belong to a wolf pack before he took up with drugs. Have you ever heard of the Tornits, great white wolves that prowl the tundra in the land of the midnight sun? They are led by an elder, Tikaani. It's a secretive pack, seldom seen. Your bloodline is half Tornit, half human. Which explains why you are recovering from the attack so quickly."

I sat stunned, shocked to the core, far too discombobulated to say one freakin' word.

"That means you were in a far better position to undergo a change to werewolf than pretty much any other human on the planet. This is good news, *thasgaidh*."

Good news? That I'm a kind of cryptid? A hybrid werewolf? I was the kind of creature the government would want to study. Suddenly, it didn't feel so good to have the shoe on the other foot. I wanted to run and hide, stay as far away from being discovered as possible. I suddenly got it.

I was instantly ashamed for my intrusion into the Creig clan world, especially since they had mostly been nice to me, if I ignored The Creig and cousin Sherry. But everyone else had known what was at stake and had still treated me like one of them. I had to make this right, tell him what I had decided. Stop torturing him for his abducting me and bringing me to Scotland. Because now I knew I would do the same thing in a heartbeat.

"I'm so sorry, Calan. I should have told you this before now. I have no intention of exposing you or your clan to the world. I'm going to destroy all my notes and make this right."

"You really mean that?" His eyes bore into mine, their liquid depths now entirely visible as he let down his defenses.

I breathed a sigh of relief that I was not too late in telling him. "Yes. I don't want you sacrificing anything else for me. You are a good man, a man your clan needs to protect them. Don't give up on your dreams. They need you—I need you."

To seal the deal, I leaned in and kissed him full on those gorgeous lips of his. A kiss that grew hotter by the second as he grabbed me and pressed his hard body up against mine. Hot lust flooded my loins and I rubbed myself against him, running my fingers through his thick locks and tugging out the tie that bound them. The scent of heather and male musk filled my nostrils, making the world tilt dizzily.

We had denied each other for far too long and now instinct took over.

He unzipped my top and made quick work of my bra, pushing it up and over my breasts, making them jut out, the nipples begging to be touched. I moaned when his lips sucked one of them into his hot mouth, drawing on that ancient chord that made me all the wetter for him.

Everything fell away, worry over family and bloodlines, drug deals and the dreaded Tribunal, leaving just us.

He dropped to his knees and pulled off my pants and underwear. His nostrils flared with lust as he touched me, my feminine musk thickening the air around us. I whimpered as he rubbed and parted the lips, his tongue driving me insane. I thrashed, my back arching off the sofa. On fire with the urgent need for release, I begged him for more. I'd never been touched a man like this before, not ever like this, with everything inside screaming for more. I dug my hands deep into his hair and pulled him closer, seeking more. He sucked hard on my clit, rolling his tongue inside me.

"I'm almost there," I whimpered. The throbbing became too much then, and I fell over the edge, waves of acute pleasure echoing through every nerve leaving me wanting more.

"Fuck me like there's no tomorrow," I growled, recovering instantly.

He slid inside me and I was lost as his hugeness stretched and bound me to him. For beautiful moments we become one, our lust and love pouring into each other. If the first time was incredible, this time it defied description. My body was no longer my own, but part of his, as his was part of mine.

"I want to claim you, make you mine, *thasgaidh*. Are you ready for this?"

"Ready? I think I was born ready for you, my love." It was the first time I'd called Calan that and his green eyes fired with an intensity of a thousand suns.

"I like the sound of that, *my love*."

"Me too. Make me yours."

He tightened his hands around my hips as he drove himself into me deeper still until I felt stretched beyond endurance just as he bit my shoulder, scenting himself in my body for all time. He licked the small wound clean and shivers raced through me.

It was done.

The room came back into focus, and it had darkened, as if the sun had already gone down. We'd made love for hours, not minutes like I'd assumed. Moonlight flooded the space and an ancient drumbeat began thrumming in my bloodstream.

"I need to run," I said with urgency.

Calan was still on top of me, still inside me, but his eyes glittered with interest. "It is time then." He nodded, as if listening to an ancient voice.

"Yes. She's calling me."

"The moon is a strong mistress."

I lightly punched his biceps. "Don't be using the 'm' word around me, mister!"

I was giddy with desire, hope and belief. And yes, love. *Sometimes you just know.* And if I were truthful, I sensed this from the very first moment I met Calan in Vegas. It had been a whirlwind courtship set against events no one could have predicted. And now, it felt like whatever it had taken to get it, it had all been worth it. A lifetime with this man wouldn't be enough.

Calan's loopy grin said it for both of us. Somehow, we were going to make *us* work.

"You're everything rolled into one, Mira. My love, my friend, my life. Will you spend it with me?"

"You asking me to marry you?"

"I am, if you'll have me?"

"A thousand times yes!"

We hugged long and hard, before the tug of the moon sent us racing down the hall out the open doorway, naked and unafraid.

Oh Goddess, that first moment, shifting to a wolf as our feet hit the ground running, nothing could have prepared me for that. The sense of the earth beating beneath my paws as they chewed up the distance, matching my mate stride for stride. Suddenly, his voice echoed in my mind and the connection was complete.

"Let's go to Wulver Cave. I want to show you something."

"Telepathy is definitely not overrated."

"No, it is not. It is everything."

I bumped against his shoulder with approval as we tore up the distance together.

"Here we are." Calan stopped moving, his attention now focused totally on me. *"You're a white wolf, like the artic tribe. Come, see yourself in the water."*

We entered the cave, side by side, up to the pool's edge. I looked down and a pair of bright blue eyes surrounded by thick white fur drew me in. I liked what I saw. A metamorphosis I could get behind. I shifted back to human again, wanting to speak aloud now. Calan did the same.

"What will your clan think, me being a different kind of wolf from them?"

"We are all wolves. Doesn't matter to the shifter kingdom what color you are, only that you follow the rules. Do no harm and protect the species."

"We need to let the Tribunal know that I will never, ever betray us."

"Are you okay with not being famous in your field? You have my word I will help you find the thing that will bring you what you want in anyway I can."

"Thank you. I'm leaning toward Billy the unicorn as my next focus."

"That I can get behind." He grew more solemn. "I want to tell you my handfasting vows right now, *thasgaidh,* share what I am thinking between just us first." He cleared his throat. "From this moment forward, I promise to be your best friend, mate and lover. To always put you first and share all I have with you. I love you with all my heart and soul, Mira."

"As I do you, Calan. I promise the same. To love you always and put you first. To love and to hold until death us do part. And even then, I will be with you always. We are one now."

Want to see more from this author? Here's a taster for you to enjoy!

Sin City Kilts: Blood of Fire
January Bain

Coming June 2023

Excerpt

"Bloody feathered tyrant!" I howled at the boisterous sounds of a rooster crowing to greet the morn before the sun was even up tearing through my wet dream like a true cock blocker. *And just when the lass was about to reveal all those luscious curves.* I yawned and checked the clock. I'd best get at it—I did have a lot on before leaving tomorrow. *Directing a movie.* My first full-length feature in Vegas, Nevada, USA. It didn't get any better than that.

I threw the covers off and made my way to the window to pull aside the drapes and check the weather. A half-moon hung smiling in the sky on its way to harvest brightness in a couple of months, the horizon growing subtly lighter to the east. *No fog this morning – the sky clear around the moon.* The distinctive sound of a church bell ringing filled my head, and I shook it in annoyance. Omens I could well do without. Nothing was going to get in my way of achieving success in my own right, not even a seer promising big life changes when I left the Highlands.

Was I taking a chance setting the movie in Vegas, even though it was the perfect location for a heist picture? Both of my older brothers were settled down happily with their new partners and lovers after returning from the City of Sin, acting too smug for words. I shook my head. *No. Not going to happen.* I wasn't one bit superstitious, was blessed with a strong mind and besides, I didn't believe in the thunderclap, at least not for me.

My brothers had just used the excuse to be with the women they wanted to be with. That old crone who'd foretold us all finding our Forever Mates in the land of desert and sage had been full of it. If she could really tell the future, she'd have won the lottery. My philosophy was to live each day to its fullest because it could be the last. *Oh, and protect your heart.*

As a wolf, I'd seen what happened to a shifter who believed in the phenomenon and was rejected by his fated mate, and it wasn't pretty. A passion that raged out of control like wildfire could only lead to one conclusion if it wasn't shared by both.

Death.

Okay, enough drama for one day. It was time to get my mind onto pleasanter occupations. I raced down the stairs two at a time, headed out for a morning run. This might be my only chance for a while. Then I should check in with Finn, my liaison in America. Finally, the farewell party planned for later. That should prove fun—a chance to let off steam before leaving Scotland.

These past few weeks I had been working harder than anyone realized, preparing to take up the reins of directorship as soon as my feet hit the ground in Nevada. I'd prove to them all that there was more to me than the playboy tag I'd been given, though there was much truth to it as well—no apologies for my sexual appetites that were as big as my…caber.

Being naked, I shifted easily, seeing myself in my mind's eye as wolf in the dimension parallel to ours, experiencing a whirlwind of incredible changes as all my energy shifted into a new form, then bouncing back into the normal world on four powerful limbs capable of great feats. That rush—that incredible sensation of letting go then acquiring incredible power—never got old.

I set off, following the trail of prey right down to the water's edge at Creig Loch, where I stood on the shoreline and looked across the deep channel. The rising sun's rays were reflected back to the heavens in a swirling mist of rainbow colors as it advanced over the edge of the world. I could only imagine capturing this on film, what a wolf sees, but it was strictly forbidden. Rule number one was never, under any circumstances, expose your pack to the human world. But it was a shame that humans weren't party to the awesomeness of the universe with blinders off.

The use of light in movie making—that was a favorite subject of mine. More particularly backlight, one of the oldest and most frequently used ways of making people look more beautiful. When focused from behind the actor or actress, making it of greater intensity than the beam hitting the actor's face, it made the subject so beautiful.

Backlit. Like walking through the woods toward a setting sun, when all the world appeared aglow. It was what made Dietrich, Garbo, Marilyn—all of them—even more glorious than they already were. It was what I intended to make good use of in my movie. What was wrong with making the world a more beautiful place?

The chase across the landscape through the glorious scented heather and moss filled me with satisfaction, reminded me of the miracle of creation and renewed my sense of commitment to my ancestors. I was more determined than ever when I turned back toward the castle for the video call with Finn, vowing to make a name for myself, come hell or high water.

* * * *

The day passed at the speed of sound and it seemed only minutes later that I was surrounded by the boisterous late-night crowd gathered in the Creigman's pub for my farewell party. I slipped a large denomination bill from my sporran and, with a wicked smile to the barman, handed the money to him to hold.

"Five hundred to the man or woman who can outdo that performance" – I nodded at the girls dancing to the music, enjoying the evening and wanting to spur on more dancing and drinking until the sun came up – "and a part in my upcoming movie as the stripper in the bar scene!"

Hoots of laughter and wild cheers erupted as the live band changed tunes to *You Can Leave Your Hat On* by Joe Cocker, a perennial favorite at the Creigman's, *the* hangout for weres in Scotland, and the perfect music for the challenge. Hell, I might even use it in *The Vegas Job*, the heist movie I was itching to direct. A well-built blue-eyed blonde was taking center stage. I'd be a hero to all the males in attendance for this one.

Does it get any better? No. I loved my life and all the perks that came with being a billionaire and a shifter. *Who wouldn't?* I had carte blanche to savor all the finer things and pursue my dreams of becoming a world-class movie director.

Sure, I love being an uncle to Lachlan's and Esme's year-old son and looked forward to him being grown enough to throw a ball with, but I wasn't ready to settle down. Sure, one day I might find the perfect woman for me, but right now my art was my focus, and if that meant nights of loneliness I would never admit to unless someone put a gun to my head, well, wasn't that what all the greats suffered to create their own vision of things?

My thoughts were interrupted by a loud chorus of "Take it off! Take it all off!"

The blonde had the crowd eating out of the palm of her hand, holding an untied bra to her chest and gyrating to the sexy beat that made the world drop away. *Now we're talking.* I loved women's bodies, with all those delicious curves. Why did they diet so much when it was curves a man craved?

Halleluiah. The blonde dropped her top and a fine pair of full breasts were revealed. The kind a man wanted to caress and kiss and suck until she was ready for a night of pleasure that ended only when the sun came up and work called. I prided myself on being a generous lover, a charming wolf who made sure my woman got off first.

"Hey, Logan, how about two for the price of one?" Ayla, one of a pair of identical twins that every man worth his salt wanted to bed, asked. She and her twin, Aileen, jumped to their feet, their ample breasts bouncing, making the current champion glare in their direction. But yeah, twin strippers in my movie…that would be hot as hades.

"Sure, give it a go, sweethearts," I said, jerking my thumb at the stage.

My cell phone rang and I glanced at the number. *Damn it.* Just when I was totally enjoying myself.

Tomorrow was soon enough to put on my serious hat and get down to business.

"Logan." I had to shout into the phone to be heard over the whistles and cheers erupting from the crowd. I wasn't the only lover of fine women in attendance.

"Mr. Creig, Finn here. Just letting you know we've found an Egyptian antiquities expert for your film."

"Good. Set up an interview for him on Sunday."

We needed the serious authority that having an expert on the subject could bring to the movie. Hopefully, he was some stuffy old geezer who would look down his bifocals at everyone—well, except me of course—and play the part well, with patches on the elbows of his out-of-date plaid jacket. That at least would save me some precious time dealing with the artifacts and preparing them for display. The complicated setting in a working casino would be ample enough challenge for the foreseeable future.

"Ah, sir, it's a woman. Comes highly recommended, I might add."

"That's all I ask." I revised the image in my mind's eyes to a middle-aged female wearing oxfords and tweed, with serious-librarian glasses perched on her nose. *Good.* As long as she came properly qualified and added a serious demeanor to my movie, she could wear any old drab outfit she wanted. It would just make it that much easier to leave her alone. I might not be superstitious, but I wasn't going to take any chances in the land of desert and sage...even if I'd admit to it out loud.

I glanced back at the twins who had taken the dance to the next level, bumping and grinding against each other with complete abandon. They were too beautiful for words—backlighting was certainly not necessary for this scene.

"Okay, ladies, you both got the part," I announced. "There'll be space set aside for you on the plane tomorrow."

I endured the squeals and shouts of glee that my words caused. Well, a man or wolf had to do what he could to keep the fairer sex happy. It must have been encoded in our DNA or maybe in our hearts, though more likely in our...*cabers* that always wanted to procreate.

Yeah, sure, someday a houseful of little Creigs running around would be great—not like I couldn't afford it. But that was a long way off in the future when I had established a successful track record in the movie business. My instincts had told me to avoid the trap of surrounding myself with women in Vegas, so I knew I wouldn't get together permanently with anyone. No, I'd treat them like the twins I'd just hired...just in case of the slim chance that the legend was true.

Yes, I was all set, I thought smugly, sitting back in my chair.

A wolf with a plan was unbeatable.

About the Author

January Bain has wished on every falling star, every blown-out birthday candle and every coin thrown in a fountain to be a storyteller. To share the tales of high adventure, mysteries, and full-blown thrillers she has dreamed of all her life. The story you now have in your hands is the compilation of a lot of things manifesting itself for this special series. Hundreds of hours spent researching the unusual and the mundane have come together to create a series that features strong women who don't take life too seriously, wild adventures full of twists and unforeseen turns, and hot complicated men who aren't afraid to take risks. She can only hope the stories of her beloved Brass Ringers will capture your imagination as much as they did hers when she wrote them.

If you are looking for January Bain, you can find her hard at work every morning without fail in her office with two furry babies trying to prove who does a better job of guarding the doorway. And, of course, she's married to the most romantic man! Who once famously replied to her inquiry about buying fresh flowers for their home every week, "Give me one good reason why not?" Leaving her speechless and knocking her head against the proverbial wall for being so darn foolish. She loves flowers.

January loves to hear from readers. You can find her contact information, website details and author profile page at https://www.totallybound.com

Sign up for our newsletter and find out about all our romance book releases, eBook sales and promotions, sneak peeks and FREE romance books!

www.ingramcontent.com/pod-product-compliance
Lightning Source LLC
LaVergne TN
LVHW090938080826
845145LV00003B/802

* 9 7 8 1 8 0 2 5 0 5 3 6 8 *